Get Your
Coventry Romances
Home Subscription NOW

And Get These
4 Best-Selling Novels
FREE:

LACEY
by Claudette Williams

THE ROMANTIC WIDOW
by Mollie Chappell

HELENE
by Leonora Blythe

THE HEARTBREAK TRIANGLE
by Nora Hampton

A Home Subscription! It's the easiest and most convenient way to get every one of the exciting Coventry Romance Novels! ...And you get 4 of them FREE!

You pay nothing extra for this convenience: there are no additional charges...you don't even pay for postage! Fill out and send us the handy coupon now, and we'll send you 4 exciting Coventry Romance novels absolutely FREE!

SEND NO MONEY, GET THESE

FOUR BOOKS FREE!

C0381

MAIL THIS COUPON TODAY TO:
**COVENTRY HOME
SUBSCRIPTION SERVICE
6 COMMERCIAL STREET
HICKSVILLE, NEW YORK 11801**

YES, please start a Coventry Romance Home Subscription in my name, and send me FREE and without obligation to buy, my 4 Coventry Romances. If you do not hear from me after I have examined my 4 FREE books, please send me the 6 new Coventry Romances each month as soon as they come off the presses. I understand that I will be billed only $11.70 for all 6 books. There are no shipping and handling nor any other hidden charges. There is no minimum number of monthly purchases that I have to make. In fact, I can cancel my subscription at any time. The first 4 FREE books are mine to keep as a gift, even if I do not buy any additional books.

For added convenience, your monthly subscription may be charged automatically to your credit card.

☐ Master Charge   ☐ Visa

Credit Card #_____

Expiration Date_____

Name_____
(Please Print)

Address_____

City_____ State_____ Zip _____

Signature_____

☐ Bill Me Direct Each Month

This offer expires Dec. 31, 1981. Prices subject to change without notice. Publisher reserves the right to substitute alternate FREE books. Sales tax collected where required by law. Offer valid for new members only.

THE RELUCTANT RIVALS

Georgina Grey

FAWCETT COVENTRY • NEW YORK

FOR
Dorothy and Jim Leys

THE RELUCTANT RIVALS

Published by Fawcett Coventry Books, a unit of CBS
Publications, the Consumer Publishing Division of CBS Inc.

Copyright © 1981 by Georgina Grey

ISBN: 0-449-50170-1

Printed in the United States of America

First Fawcett Coventry printing: March 1981

10 9 8 7 6 5 4 3 2 1

One

"The nuisance is, my dear," Sir George Tigford said fretfully, "that you are too good by half. It will not do, you know. It will not do at all."

Belinda inclined her head dutifully. "I am sure that it will not, Papa, since you say so," she replied. "But it seems to be my nature."

They were sitting on either side of the fireplace in the little sitting room where Sir George liked to take his tea, making a pleasant domestic picture, or so Kate Harrison thought as she stood beside the window. And, indeed, everything would be at harmony in the household she had joined just a few weeks ago were it not for the fact that Sir George saw the need to make a constant fuss and bother over the fact that his daughter was not the *femme fatale* he wanted her to be.

Still, Kate thought, her uncle's eccentricity in

this regard should not keep her from remembering that he had been gracious enough to offer to attend to the details of her coming-out. It was particularly obliging of him since he was a widower like her own father whose duties as a squire kept him in the country. No doubt it was troublesome for a gentleman to see to his own daughter's introduction to Society, and to have taken on the responsibility of a niece as well showed singular good nature on his part.

"It will not make a mite of difference whether I have one or two chits to attend to," he had written to Kate's father more than a month ago. "Certainly I am well aware that this should be a woman's business, but there you are. I am quite willing to make sacrifices to see Belinda launched, but I will not go so far as to take a wife simply to help me do it. Besides that, Lady Prudence, whom I am certain that you must remember, has been good enough to offer me her help regarding the ordering of gowns and other frippery of that sort. So tell your Kate to pack her things and come up to London at once. With any luck both she and her cousin will have made a fine match by the time the Season is over. Mind that if they do not it will not be for want of trying on my part."

Kate considered her uncle fondly as he continued to fuss over the patient Belinda. Sir George was a large, ruddy-faced gentleman who filled his wing chair to capacity. The club wig which he wore at home was made of stiff black horsehair and featured a great roll above each ear, and he was dressed in the pink of fashion in a blue frock coat with a black velvet turned down collar and buff pantaloons which were cut short enough to show a fine turn of white-stockinged calf. But the grandest thing was his long waistcoat fancifully embroidered in reds and greens and bisected by a thick gold chain which held his watch.

In contrast to her father, Belinda was extraordinarily petite, a pretty sprite in her pink sack dress with a white frilled tippet filling her low-necked bodice and a *dormeuse* bonnet caught about with a pink bow which showed only a hint of her golden curls. Her expression was one of such extraordinary good nature that Kate thought Sir George was doomed to disappointment in his attempts to turn his daughter into someone to fit his conception of a young lady of the *beau monde*.

"You know, I only want the best for you, my dear," he said ponderously. "And for that you must add a certain fillip to your behavior. Kate's dry humor will serve her well, I fancy. But you are too even dispositioned, too honest and direct, too lacking in surprise. In a word, my dear, you need a certain cachet."

"I will try, Papa," Belinda said earnestly. "But I do not think I can ever be the sort of siren you have in mind."

"Pah! It is the simplest of things, I'm sure, Child. Indeed it must be or so many ladies would not play at it. Consider an example of your behavior. The other evening at Lady Bentknees, you recall, Lord Pimpton tried to make a conquest of you, I observed."

"Why, he acted very strangely, to be sure,"

7

Belinda said with an innocence which Kate knew was no pretense. "At first I thought he must be in his cups for he pranced around so on his high-heeled shoes and winked and blinked in such a peculiar way that I could not think of any other answer."

"He is a dandy, gel!" her father declared with such a degree of indignation that Belinda gave a start and looked at him quite anxiously. "A macaroni, if you will, for I believe he is a member of that club. He was flirting with you, miss, and you could only stand and stare at him as though he had two heads."

"But Papa, he did look so very odd," Belinda protested. "His wig was a foot high, at least, and there were three patches cut in the shape of stars on his face and I declare his nosegay was large enough to make a bride's bouquet."

Her father took a deep, slow breath. "But that is the *way* of things," he persisted. "It is the fashion, Child, and fashion never is absurd. Come, Kate, do you not agree?"

"I will take your word on it, sir," Kate replied, "although it is a maxim which is difficult to remember at times."

"At least *you* are amused by the foibles of Society," Sir George declared. "Amused and dare to show it! But Belinda acts as though she were paying a call at Bedlam every time she attends an entertainment, damme if she don't."

"But it is all so strange, Papa," Belinda said. "First we are living quietly in the country and then, when I turn eighteen, we must come direct

8

to London and join the *haut ton*. If someone had told me what it would be like here while we were still in Kent, I never would have believed it.

"It is as fresh to Kate as you, miss," Sir George fretted. "So you think that Kate would have made such a faux pas as you did when Lady Hervey asked if you would like the name of her *friseur*."

Belinda blushed. "I only meant to be quite honest, Papa," she said. "And it is true that I do not think my head would support such a great weight. Why, I heard it said that she has had to have the roof of her sedan chair raised quite two feet to accommodate her wigs."

"Faugh!" Sir George exclaimed, throwing up his hands. "What shall I do with the child, Kate?"

Although Kate was only a year older than her cousin, her uncle had taken to consulting her at every turn although she had assured him often enough that this was all as new to her as to Belinda. But he would only call her sensible and persist until she had given her opinion.

So she came forward now, a slim, graceful girl with a flood of auburn curls escaping from her frilled mobcap, and skin as fair and smooth as cream to make a contrast with the rich brown of her eyes.

"Why, I should think it would satisfy if she were just to do and say the exact opposite of what occurs to her," she said wryly. "Since Belinda can always trust to her impulse to be honest, it should be a simple matter to turn everything about and lie instead. I only use that for one example."

"La, Kate!" Belinda cried. "You are mocking me!"

"No," the girl replied. "Quite the contrary, I assure you. Laugh when you think that you should cry, smile when it seems time to frown, lie when the truth might be awkward and sometimes when it might not. Is not that the way of it, Uncle?"

"That's doing it a bit brown perhaps," Sir George replied, looking up at his niece through his thick eyebrows as though not certain whether he was being made game of or not. "But you are right in saying that the gel should never follow her impulse since it will lead her wrong every time. And that includes the sort of gentleman whom you ought to favor."

Belinda threw Kate an anxious look, for in midnight conversations they had decided that in his efforts to do the right thing Sir George might become too enthusiastic by far.

"He seems to have conjured up an image of the sort of gentleman that I would like to marry," she had told Kate the night of her arrival. "He should be rich and titled and what Papa calls 'a gay, young blade,' although what that means I do not dare to think."

And then both of them had taken turns at brushing one another's hair and making confidences, for although they had known one another all their lives, they had never lived together as sisters.

"I do not think that I could marry a man I was not fond of," Belinda said. "But poor Papa will be quite frantic if I am not settled and taken care of by the time the Season is over. He has quite set his heart on it."

"But surely the choice of the gentleman you will spend the remainder of your life with is more important than Uncle's feelings," Kate had protested, although she suspected that stronger arguments even than that would be necessary to make a rebel of her cousin. And yet she could not simply stand aside and let Sir George bully her into marrying someone who suited his fancy, gay young blades not being much in Belinda's line apparently. It had been at that moment that Kate had vowed to protect her cousin in any way she could.

"The time has come for me to give you some direction, child," Sir George was saying now with the arch benevolence which he liked to assume when being particularly paternal.

Since she had seldom heard him doing anything except giving directions since she had come to London, Kate paid particular attention.

"I know you only want to be polite to Lady Prudence," her uncle said, patting the hands which Belinda had neatly folded in her lap, "and I would be the first to say we owed her a debt of gratitude. But we must not pretend that her youngest son is anything but profoundly ineligible. I know that for some reason which I have never been able fathom, Lady Prudence thinks the sun rises and sets with him, but he is a sullen fellow in my opinion, and he has no prospects. As youngest son with three brothers older than he, there is no question of the title coming to him and, from what Lady Prudence tells me, there will be little enough money to divide when the lads inherit."

"But Papa," Belinda began with such an open look of misery on her face that she gave herself away at once.

"Aha!" Sir George exclaimed. "Then I was not mistaken to think you had begun to fancy him! He is not the gentleman for you, my dear. Why, 'pon my soul, your mother would never forgive me if I let you go to such a fellow! Lady Prudence will understand when I have explained it to her. No doubt she did not realize that she was pushing you in his direction."

Now that it was too late to lead him off the scent, Belinda began to try, but with no skill in manipulation she was doomed to fail. Certainly it was not the time to disclose the fact that she had taken to calling Lady Prudence's pride and joy Fitz, nor was Sir George impressed when she protested that she thought of him only as a friend. And when she declared that she had only been his partner twice the evening before at Lady Sweetwell's and it appeared that Sir George had not seen her take the floor with him at all, she was in hotter water than she had been when she had started.

"Damme, gel, you'd better leave off your defense before you force a conviction!" Sir George shouted. "So it is Fitz, is it, and only two minuets! Phaugh, it is just as well, I see, that I am taking matters in my hands."

Kate drew close to Belinda's chair and placed a comforting hand on her shoulder. Once they were alone again she must remember to explain carefully to Belinda that, for her own protection, she should learn the basic techniques of dissembling to her father. Now that his eyes had been so firmly drawn to young Fitz Ronhugh, he would doubtless make further meets between the young couple as difficult as possible and, whereas another sort of girl might be spurred on by barriers, Kate knew Belinda, obedient as ever, would never think to scale them.

"The fact of the matter is," Sir George was saying now, "that I have found the perfect gentleman for you, my pet. A young man after my own heart."

"Please, Papa," Belinda murmured, "he is not a gay young blade, I hope!"

"Why, what if he is, my dear? What if he is? Yes, indeed, he is a scamp and soundrel, a perky fellow with a fine handle to his name and fortune enough for three! No doubt he would have been married off long ago, if some young lady had been as artful as you are going to be!"

"I do not want to be artful!" Belinda wailed. "And even if I did I do not know how!"

"You will follow my directions, miss!" Sir George said, taking snuff from the back of his hand with a certain air of majesty. "I was a gay blade in my youth, you know. That is why I find the fellow so appealing, no doubt. Yes! Yes! I was the very devil before your mother caught me. Ah, your dear mother was a very clever young lady, my dear. I cannot fancy why, since you have her looks, you do not have her ways. Why, she could scheme her way around me before I even knew that anything was in the wind. It has been a long time, of course, since those days, and I may have forgotten a detail here, a detail there. But I remember the gist of it."

Belinda looked at him with so much mute appeal in her blue eyes that Kate did not know how he could resist her. But once Sir George got a notion in his head it blinded him to everything but what he wanted to see, which, in this case was not his daughter's misery.

"Damme if it won't be a lark!" he declared. "Put some spirit into things, at last. Dash it, gel, but it's a tedious thing for an old gentleman like me to thumb through envelopes the entire morning, trying to decide which entertainments would serve you best. Now we need only those the marquess attends. If I know Dev, he will choose only the jollier ones!"

"Dev!" Kate exclaimed. "Pray, what is his full name, Uncle, and where did you meet him?"

Sir George took another sniff of snuff and sneezed twice loudly. "Why, I knew him as a lad when his father would bring him to White's to watch the play. He was a scamp then and when I met him again in Virginia last year, he seemed a jolly fellow still. His father had plantations in the colonies, you understand. Dev was thinking then that he might stay, or so he said. But then things started turning awkward. He tells me that it may come to war in the end. But that's another story. The fact is that Devereau Gilcrest is back and that he has inherited both title and fortune since he left England. And you shall have him, my dear Belinda. I am quite set on it. That

14

scoundrel Dev little thinks that he is about to pit his wits against mine."

"You speak as though your daughter were a pawn in a chess game, sir," Kate said. She had gone very pale and her brown eyes were startled, as though they had just seen something quite unexpected. "I hope you will not think it rude of me to beg you to change your mind before this game is begun."

Two

"Something is wrong, Kate. I know it. Why you went ever so pale when Papa spoke of that gentleman he met in Virginia."

"That was because it was so stuffy in the sitting room," Kate told her cousin. "And besides I cannot bear the smell of snuff. But I will be better here in the garden. Come. Let us cut some roses for the table."

There was no difficulty in deceiving Belinda, particularly as she was bound up in her own affairs and she was soon clipping away at the rose bushes with a troubled look in her blue eyes as Kate held the basket and the soft, spring sunlight made a dapple of the scene. Kate's thoughts, too, were sadly at war with the beauty all around them, as she thought of the first time she had met Devereau Gilcrest, the gentleman she now thought of as Dev.

She had been a girl of fifteen when he had first come roistering into her life. It had been a brisk day in October with the fields in stubble, and she had been riding her chestnut mare across the south meadow when she had seen a hunt of some fifteen to twenty gentlemen in their pink coats with the hounds baying in front of them come thundering by. And, because she yearned for a little excitement and knew a little thicket where foxes often went to cover, Kate had spurred her own horse to a gallop.

Nothing would have come of it, perhaps, had she been more properly attired, but because she did not care for the sidesaddle and because her father indulged her in a hundred little ways, she was outfitted in her favorite riding costume which consisted of a pair of buckskin breeches and a shabby, blue jacket which had once belonged to her older brother Tom. As for her hair, it was tucked under one of the squire's old cocked hats, and so it was that when Dev had first caught sight of her he had mistaken her for a boy.

The circumstances of their first meeting had been equally at odds with propriety for he had been lying in the stubble beside his horse which was cropping away at the grass beside a high, stone wall, apparently oblivious of the fact that his master's right foot was twisted in the stirrup.

Even before Kate could slide down from her horse, she was treated to a series of oaths which, since she spent considerable time in her father's stables, failed to shock her, but rather won her admiration for the remarkable variety, not to mention color, of the phrases which the stranger employed.

Only when she had released his booted foot from the stirrup did she have a chance to observe him closer, and upon doing so found him to be handsome in a wild, dark way. The dark eyes were sardonic and the cheekbones high. His complexion was bronzed as though he spent a good deal of his time outdoors, and his mouth was thin and somehow sensitive. For most of the first five minutes of their meeting, however, she was treated to little more than a view of the top of his dark head as he occupied himself with rubbing his leg furiously, still continuing to curse.

The necessity to get his right boot off before the ankle was swollen too badly turned his attention to Kate again, although he scarcely looked at her before demanding that she help him.

"Damme, what are you about?" he demanded as, facing him, she began to tug at the offending boot. "That's not the way of it. Turn your back on me, boy, and bend!"

Kate was too startled to protest, and so, placing herself astride the leg, she bent and felt the pressure of his other foot against her back. Crimson with humiliation, she still turned herself to the task only to be rewarded with a final push when the boot finally slid off, a push which landed her, face first, in a muddy patch left over from the rain the night before.

He laughed then. She might have forgiven him anything but that. Wiping the mud off her face

19

with the sleeve of her jacket, she remounted her horse and slapped the reins.

"See here," the stranger cried out then, "I'll be blasted if you don't intend to go off and leave me lying here. You know that I can't manage on my own. The ankle's wrenched badly, but if you will help me get to my feet, I may be able to mount. Dash it, but don't you look a sight! Still, I didn't see the mud. I can promise you that."

Kate had had every intention of standing on her dignity, but she had sense of humor enough to see herself in his eyes. Then, too, she desperately did not want him to know she was a girl, and the mud was helpful as part of her disguise. And then he laughed, and it was clear he was in pain although he clenched his teeth against it when it came.

But still she dared not speak, knowing that her voice might betray her. As a consequence, her only response was to shrug and jump down from her horse again to provide him with the shoulder he required. It was necessary to expend every bit of strength she had to support him until he managed to pull himself into the saddle.

The pain of the effort left him white-faced, but he said nothing, clenching the pommel of his saddle until the agony had retreated and he could offer Kate his thanks.

"Ought to put some more meat on your bones, lad," the stranger said with an attempt at laughter. "It doesn't do for a boy to be so slight. Now, if you'll just point out the closest way back to Fandrill Hall, I'll not trouble you any longer. If

I'd had a notion that Felix meant to provide me with a horse which prefers to run through walls instead of jumping over them, I would have paid my visit elsewhere."

The time had come when Kate knew she must talk and take the risk which accompanied letting him hear the sound of her voice.

"It's a longish way to the Hall," she muttered, staring at the ground, "and hard riding, too. I can take you to the village, if you like, and see you to the doctor's doorstep."

She almost hoped he would refuse, although she knew that if he insisted on riding to Fandrill Hall he might become light in the head and fall. But then she told herself that if she were clever, she might be able to see the stranger provided for without disclosing the fact that the mudstained face she had presented him was that of a girl and not a boy. Although why it mattered she did not know. After all, boy or girl, she was no more than a child to him.

" 'Lead on, Macduff!' " he replied with a crooked smile. "Which brings to mind your real name. What is it, pray?"

In a panic, Kate chose her initials.

"K.H.!" the stranger exclaimed. "What did your parents mean to do? Did they intend to make a gudgeon of you, some sort of laughingstock?"

In as few words as she could manage, Kate explained that it was only a nickname, at which the stranger quieted a bit and announced that although his full name was Devereau Gilcrest, his friends called him Dev.

21

"And since I hereby nominate you as my friend, that is what you must call me, too," he announced and fell at once, as their horses slowly climbed the hill, into a song so ribald that Kate was glad of the mud to hide her blushing.

Never, she thought, had she seen such a carefree gentleman. Even though he was clearly in pain, he appeared to be in high spirits, as though he did not known any other way to live. No sooner was the song finished that he would tell her of his plans to go to Virginia where his father, whom he referred to dryly as 'his lordship' owned a vast plantation. For awhile, he grew almost lyrical as he painted a vision of vast spaces and endless forests. Indeed his enthusiasm was so contagious that, even though Kate knew very little about the British colonies in America, she could almost see what he was describing.

"The fact is, we're growing stale here," he said and his voice was suddenly somber. Turning to look at him, Kate saw that his face was grave.

"A fellow gets tired of drinking and roistering after a while," he muttered as though he were speaking to himself. "Felix and the others I was with . . . Someone must have seen me come a cropper, but did they stop? Not bloody likely. The fact is, most of them drank enough of that stirrup cup before we started to make it likely that they haven't even missed me yet."

After that he remained silent, clearly lost in his own thoughts, until they reached the outskirts of the village and the doctor's old half-timbered house with its upper story hanging over the road.

"Pull that," Kate said, indicating the bell which hung by the door. "He'll see to everything. And now goodbye."

"Not before I shake your hand, lad," he told her, leaning forward in the saddle to do so despite the pain it cost him. "And here is something for your troubles."

Before she had realized that it was a coin he had tossed her, Kate had caught it. It was a guinea and she wanted more than anything to give it back. But he was already tugging on the bell and, knowing that the physician would recognize her, she thanked him and said goodbye.

"Goodbye, *Dev*," he had corrected her, grinning, but just then the door had begun to open and Kate was forced to gallop off. But to herself she whispered what was to become part of her private litany, "Goodbye, Dev."

And now to have him turn up this way! And her uncle had called him scamp and scoundrel, albeit in a fond way. And, after dreaming of him all these years, Kate was, no doubt, expected to help Belinda lure a gentleman she did not care a whit for. But at that thought Kate stopped herself. It might be that up to now her cousin had been content to be paid attention to by Fitz, but it might happen that when she saw Dev she would find, as Kate had, that it was difficult to forget him.

Telling herself that speculation was of no use at all, Kate surveyed the facts which were, to wit, that quite unknown to the gentleman in question, she had met Devereau Gilcrest four years ago,

23

and that the memory of that meeting had played about the fringes of her mind ever since. However, four years had passed since then and, as she was unlikely to meet him again either wearing men's clothing or with mud smeared on her face, it was improbable that he would recognize her. Add to that the fact that if he had eluded the grasps of as many ladies as her uncle had implied, he was quite unlikely either to succumb either to Belinda's reluctant banishments or to notice a red-haired young lady straight from the country.

Practicality having offered some relief, Kate aroused herself to the fact that her cousin was no longer busy with her shears, and that a tear was wandering down her cheek.

"Oh, Kate," she wailed as she felt the comforting hand on her arm. "Do you expect Papa really means to make me do it? I mean to say I never fancied myself a Circe, and as for Mother having been one I will not believe it! How can it please him so to think she schemed and planned to catch him?"

"No doubt it satisfies his pride," Kate suggested softly. "I do not mean that as a rebuke, you know. Not even as a criticism. But gentlemen must have their myths about the ladies and I think that is one of them. They think of themselves as prizes, don't you know."

"You make it sound so harmless," Belinda said, "but I think he means to give me tactics as though this were a war that is about to be fought, and he the officer and I the foot soldier."

Kate thought that her cousin had chosen her metaphors well for, if not a war, surely Sir George planned to have a game. And for what motives? Because he wanted to see his daughter married. Because he wanted to put an end to the nightly soirees and entertainments that constituted the questionable rewards of "coming out." Because he saw something of himself in the young marquess. All these were reasons that Kate could understand. But when Sir George decided to make a game of it, he had lost her sympathy entirely.

"It may be," Kate said tentatively, "that he is not serious."

"Papa is always serious when it comes to finding me a husband. Why, I have not heard him make a joke about it once since we came to London. I shall feel like such a fool, I know I will."

Kate took the shears and cut a handsome orange tea rose. Certainly it would be wrong of her to urge Belinda to rebel against her father for, even though she would rather have remained in the country, he had been very kind to her. Besides, how could she be certain of her motives? Or why could Sir George not have chosen someone beside Dev?

"Do you expect Papa will want me to wear my gowns low cut and pile my hair over a frame?" Belinda fretted. "I do not dare to think how he will expect me to act. Quite shamelessly, I imagine. And even you made a joke of how I should act the opposite of what I feel!"

Kate caught her cousin by the waist and kissed her. "It was nothing but a joke!" she cried. "Besides, I thought to make your father see how absurd it was to expect you to act anything but naturally."

"He sees nothing absurd in it," Belinda said dolefully. "And I am always so obedient. It suits me to be so. He has already told me that I am to see nothing more of Fitz. Oh dear, I cannot bear it!"

"Why, I have just thought of something which may prove the saving grace!" Kate declared. "Your father still has Lady Prudence to contend with. He will have to tell her of his plan and I am certain she will make a formidable opponent to it. You know that she wants you for Fitz. And she is a manipulator of the first water."

"Oh, do you think that she will really help me?" Belinda cried, her eyes taking on a sparkle.

"From what I have seen of her ladyship, I would think of it as a certainty," Kate replied. "Yes, Cousin, I think it possible the fur will fly when your papa tells her what he intends to do."

Three

Lady Prudence was a baroness which, in her own words, ". . . makes me sound so common. That is to say it has a frightfully foreign ring about it, don't you think?"

And, of course, no one could blame her for being condescending, for her father had been the Duke of Fairbow with vast holdings in the north, not to mention considerable property in London and a genealogical line which took the family back to the Norman conquest, all of which had made for considerable awkwardness when she had chosen to fall in love with Lord Mancer, a baron from Tevtree, which was no more nor less than a small market town in Sussex.

Even as a girl Lady Prudence possessed a forceful personality, and in the battle which ensued on her announcement that she would marry whom she liked, it was the duke her father who had emerged bloodied and beaten. But he had had the pleasure, at least, of leaving her a pittance in his will, and so it was that twenty-five years later Lady Prudence faced the world with four grown sons, only one of whom had even the prospect of a title to help him find a bride. As for the baron, he preferred to remain in the country where he spent the days with cronies of his youth, failed fellows like himself, who liked above all things to spend their days in sport which allowed them to kill nearly everything that moved.

Lady Prudence, however, being of a more practical turn of mind was determined to refill the family coffers by arranging advantageous marriages for her sons who, listed in order of age, were Frederick, Frank, Fairbanks and Fitzgerald, ordinarily called Fitz. The brothers had more in common than the letter *F* to their names, all having been molded to a considerable degree by a strongminded mother whose voice had drummed so ceaselessly in their ears for so many years that they scarcely knew where their thinking began and hers left off. Other than that, they were personable enough young men who viewed their lives as something to be molded by their mother into whatever shape she fancied.

For Frederick, this Season, Lady Prudence had chosen a certain Miss Drusella Davenport, whose father's fortune made from shrewd trading on the 'change more than made up for his daughter's singular lack of good looks. Since this was Frederick's fourth Season on the marriage mart, and his mother was growing impatient in a way which did little to improve what was, at best, an uneven disposition, the young gentleman had consented to court Miss Davenport with an ardor which he was far from feeling.

As for Frank, he tended to be foppish in his ways and spent more time before his mirror than many a young lady of her acquaintance, or so Lady Prudence liked to observe when she was out of temper with him. The single advantage to this streak of narcissism, however, was the fact that he cared very little who his mother's choice of the year might be for him. When he was twenty she had sent him in pursuit of the daughter of a marquess who had been distinguished only by such raucous laughter as could make an entire room full of people stop their conversation and turn to look at her. When he was twenty-one, Lady Prudence's choice had been Lady Phoebe Philmount who boasted an easy manner and a badly tarnished reputation, and the next year he had been directed to woo and win The Honorable Letitia Lightfoot who would have been a prize in all respects, had it only been that she had ever been able to master the rudiments of reading and writing. Having been branded with three years of failure, Frank was being strongly urged by his mama to spend less time on his cravats and patches and dedicate more hours to composing the compliments with which he should win a lady's heart.

Fairbanks, being next to the youngest, promised well for, although his prize of the year before had got away, she had so nearly given him her hand that her furious papa had rushed her out of London to the family estate in Northumberland, and finding even that distance not far enough to calm his fears, had subsequently removed the poor girl to the highland area of Scotland, where she had spent an unhappy summer coming to the conclusion that if it meant all this bother and inconvenience dear Fairbanks must be forgotten.

But it was for Fitz that Lady Prudence had the highest hopes this Season, for she had no sooner come to London with her little brood than she had encountered her old friend Sir George Tigford, and not only found him in possession of a need for her assistance but of a daughter as well, a pretty little thing who had caught Fitz's fancy at once. Having first determined that Sir George's fortune remained intact, and that it would indeed be passed on to his only child, Lady Prudence was only too eager to see to Belinda's gowns and such, and it was remarkable the number of shopping expeditions on which Fitz accompanied them.

So it was with something less than enthusiasm that the baroness heard Sir George's plan. However, she was clever enough not to make an immediate protest. Instead she made a retreat to the crumbling, decrepit house just off Portman Square which constituted the last of her husband's London properties, and sent off a note to her old nurse, for whom her father had provided more generously, as things turned out, than he had for his daughter. Nanny Benbow had invested her money in a snug little property close to the Park where she could spend her declining years absorbed, at a decent distance, in the affairs of the *haut monde,* an interest which she had pursued for years with what might reasonably be called a passion. As a result no one, not even the notorious gossip-monger Lady Latchlip herself, knew more savory scandal than kindly old Nanny Benbow; and it was Lady Prudence's ardent hope that among her old nurse's gems and jewels she would find something suitable with which to tarnish the name of a certain young marquess.

Lady Prudence's London house offered little to distract her from what she hoped was a temporary disappointment. It had been decorated by her husband's paternal grandmother, a lady who seemed to have spent her entire life doing needlework. As a result there was scarcely a surface, be it wall or furniture in the shabby rooms, which was not covered with faded and decaying embroidery, petit point or what had been called 'stump work.' In the sitting room where she awaited the arrival of her old nurse Lady Prudence could, if she liked, study either one of two petit point panels, the first portraying the visit of the Queen of Sheba to Solomon and the other, a masterful albeit nearly indistinguishable representation of Cain slaying Abel. Once, no doubt, the colors had glowed, but now all was reduced to a dull greenish-gray which, covering as it did the chest in one corner and the front of a cabinet in another, not to mention serving as a border for three mirrors, thus created an awful gloom which the huge mahogany chairs of the Lion Period, with legs carved in such a manner as to make them seem to crouch, did little to dispel.

Lady Prudence could properly be called a magnificent specimen of a woman, having inherited her father's physique if not his fortune. Nearly six feet in height, she dwarfed her four sons and carried on her face the distinguished aquiline nose and the protruding eyes which had for centuries distinguished the Fairbow family. These features appeared on her sons' faces in a diluted form, her husband's blood being just strong enough to modify but not to change. In spite of this, its potency seemed to increase with each successive offspring, with the result that Fitz, the youngest, could boast quite passable good looks.

As she waited for her old nurse to join her, Lady Prudence plotted her course. Her first temptation, when Sir George had given her the news regarding his ambitions for his daughter, had been to ride over the notion roughshod. Did Belinda care for the fellow, she might have demanded. Of course she did not, having never met him. Was it likely that such a fellow as Sir George had described would throw his heart over the wall for such an innocent as Belinda who, although quite pretty enough, was not a raving beauty? But before she could speak, Sir George had made her privy to his plan to plot maneuvers which Belinda could employ to win the young marquess's attention. At first Lady Prudence had been tempted to treat the idea with the scorn it probably deserved, but then she thought that might make Sir George even more obdurate, given his nature. But the greatest test of her restraint had come when, with the subtlety of a rhinoceros, Sir George had proposed that, since he did not want Belinda much distracted during the crucial days ahead, he would like to see Fitz elsewhere than at her side.

And so she had seethed in quiet impatience to take her departure. Granted that once she was in her carriage, rented for the Season, she pounded the leather cushion of the seat until the dust flew. The worst thing about the matter was that Sir George might be successful if, as he said, Lord Gilcrest was a fellow after his own heart and very like him as a youth. Lady Prudence had not raised four boys for nothing, and she knew that it was only necessary to devise the proper scheme to make them bend to her will. If Sir George happened to hit upon the proper formula, no doubt the young marquess might succumb as well.

It had been then that she had thought of her old nurse with her passion for scandal, old or new. She was familiar enough with Nanny Benbow's ways to know that she even kept records of the events which came to her attention, events which might be recorded by the papers but which had no special meaning until strung together in the proper way. It might, for instance, seem to indicate nothing in particular if it was reported in the *Morning Post* that Lady Nearly had gone to Bath to take the waters, but, if one were clever enough to note the next day in the *London Gazette* that Lord Bevy had done the same, leaving his wife in London, and if this sequence of events involving the same two characters had occurred often enough, certain conclusions might be drawn. And Nanny Benbow's conclusions were very clever indeed.

Lady Prudence would have gladly gone to Nanny Benbow, rather than asking the old woman to come to her, had it not been for the fact that her father's former retainer relished every excuse to get out and about and was inclined to be insulted if deprived of the opportunity. It was understood, at least between her and her former ward, that for every bit of information extended on her part a fair exchange be made, and Lady Prudence was scowling in her attempt to remember the worst thing she had heard about any one of her friends recently when a hired sedan chair was set down outside the window to announce the arrival of her guest.

Nanny Benbow's face bore a strong resemblance to a withered apple which had somehow managed to maintain the first, rosy flush of its youth. She wore tin-rimmed spectacles which she was in the habit of allowing to slip to the very end of her short nose, and she preferred to dress in the fashion of an earlier age in a sacque gown of a neat lilac dimity, gathered in great swoops over a hooped petticoat. Lady Prudence was never less than generous in her good wishes for her old nurse, but she often wondered what the duke her father would have thought if he had known that the comfortable allowance he had left his faithful retainer would be spent on a little house in London and dressmakers willing to outfit the old woman in the mode of her girlhood. It was as though after a lifetime of service Mrs. Benbow had decided on a final bacchanalia of sorts.

As she waited for the old woman to be shown into the shabby sitting room by Harry, an accommodating young fellow who not only drove the hired carriage but doubled, when the occasion demanded, as footman and butler as well, Lady Prudence reflected on the fact that, as news of her clever ways with scandal were voiced about, Nanny Benbow might become much in demand. True, of course, that because of her past station as a servant she could never be accepted as a full member of the *haut ton*, but that had never been her desire. All that she had ever wanted was to hear as much fresh scandal daily as was possible, and she took no interest in any news, no matter how astonishing, which did not concern her social superiors. This made her, Lady Prudence reflected, an eccentric snob indeed, but it was not her part to criticize. If servants from every great house in London brought Nanny Benbow information for a fee, then it was to the good of all concerned that there be a market for it, a market Lady Prudence was determined to provide.

Remembering her old nurse's sweet tooth, Lady Prudence had told Harry to serve sweetmeats, and when the unlikely old creature had wobbled her uncertain way into the room and been settled in a chair, the boy had been smart about his duties, and having served the old lady before, provided her with a large glass of ratafia as well. Furthermore, being a clever lad, he did not bother to return the decanter to the table so that he could, quite literally, be on hand when Nanny Benbow held out her glass for more, which she did with extraordinary promptitude.

"And now, my dear," she said to Lady Prudence, having drained the second glass and leaned forward with her goldheaded cane clutched just below her chin, "what is it?"

Since they understood one another so completely, there was no need for preludes, prefaces or preliminaries. The baroness rose to pace the musty room as she explained matters, and her old nurse listened carefully. Lady Prudence had not changed from her walking costume, a formidable affair of dark green sarsenet which, being a polonaise gown had a train trimmed with black braid. And since she had not even removed her stiff-brimmed hat with its three large feathers, she appeared to be rather more than life-sized, even to Nanny Benbow, who even to this day would sometimes call her erstwhile charge a 'great girl.'

"I believe I have a notation or two on Sir George Tigford," Nanny Benbow said when Lady Prudence had finished. Age had made her voice scratchy, and she spoke at a pitch well above normal because she was growing deaf.

"Wife was a bit of a gad, I believe, although there were never any serious rumors. Why, it must be quite ten years since she died! It was her lungs that took her, as I recall."

"You really are a marvel, Nanny," Lady Prudence declared. "How you remember all those odds and ends I'll never know. I remember when I was a girl your telling me such stories of Society. Why, I thought you must be making them up. Of course, after I had come out, I realized it was all quite true. But that is by the by. The important thing is Lord Gilcrest's reputation."

"It may be a bad sign, gel, that I can't bring his name to mind straight off," Nanny Benbow said, wagging her mobcapped head. Age had given her certain privileges, among them being her choice of address. Certainly 'gel' was scarcely the term which would have come to most lips when confronted with Lady Prudence, nor would she have accepted the familiarity from anyone but her old nurse.

"He's certain to have done any number of shameless things," the baroness declared. "Sir George called him a scamp and a rascal himself."

"It puzzles me why you should think that any account of something shameful in the young man's past should give this Sir George of yours any pause to speak of," Nanny Benbow retorted. "He knows that he's a scamp already, and there's an end to it."

Lady Prudence shook her head until the three feathers in her hat fell into a quaver. "I could tell from Sir George's voice that he did not mean anything very bad by 'scamp' and 'scoundrel.' A bit of gambling, perhaps, and general roistering about, but nothing of a serious nature. You know the sort of thing I mean. Maidens deserted. I do not need to elaborate to *you*."

"Indeed you do not, gel," Nanny Benbow replied with a broad smile which revealed a considerable expanse of toothless gums. But Lady Prudence was used to her and did not notice, any more than she did the old lady's strangely antique costumes.

"Then if you can accommodate me I will be very grateful," she said. "This means so much to Fitz, you understand. Dear boy, he is quite taken with his Belinda, and I intend that he shall have her."

Four

Lady Finespun's entertainments were known to be among the most exclusive in the city, and, as a consequence, when each of her guests entered the grand ballroom to the accompaniment of the liveried footman's sonorous pronouncement of their name, there was a little flutter and a flurry as conversations stopped and everyone craned their necks to see who was now being allowed the privilege of joining them.

"The first thing to be accomplished is that you must recognize the gentleman," Sir George declared, negotiating his daughter into a position beside the musicians' platform which commanded a fine view of the door. "As soon as you hear his name announced, sharpen your eyes."

"But I thought you intended to introduce me to Lord Gilcrest, Papa," Belinda said, wrinkling her pretty face into a mask of perplexity. "And if I am introduced to him I will know who he is. I mean to say . . ."

"What a muddle she does make of things," Sir George said to Kate, speaking over his daughter's head. "Now listen to me, Belinda. I have decided not to introduce you after all."

"Then you mean to forget your plan, sir!" Belinda exclaimed with delight. "You do not know how happy you have made me!"

Grumbling, Sir George prevented her from hugging him in her excess of pleasure. "That is not the way of it either, gel," he declared. "Can you not be quiet long enough for me to explain myself?"

Kate was forced to look away in order to hide her amusement. Sir George had been so full of plans these past few days, each one more complicated than the next, that she had come to take his project less seriously. Indeed she had applied her sense of the practical to the situation in general with so much energy that she now was able to laugh at herself for making such a romance out of a childhood encounter. Granted that to her country maiden's eyes the handsome stranger had seemed to march directly out of the pages of a book, but she was older now, and quite prepared to see him make such an outrageous display as the fops with their powder and patches and their posturings. Had he not told her himself that when he was in England he had too much to do with the wrong sort of gentlemen? When he came through that door she might not even recognize him. Certainly he would never recognize her.

"I intend for you to meet him, chit!" Sir George was saying. "But I do not want him to think I planned it. Dev is a shrewd chap, and he might guess what I had in mind if I made a fuss and bother over you. Well, well, I am too clever for that, I assure you. He will happen on you. I will explain myself in a moment. And later, when I see that he has made your acquaintance, I will not be pleased!"

"But Papa!" Belinda cried. "That is unfair surely. Why should you be displeased to have me know him when you have gone to such pains to make the meeting come about? I declare, you are making me so very miserable that I am afraid I will cry at any moment."

"Cry!" Sir George exclaimed. "Certainly not, my lady! Not if lightning should split this roof and decimate half of the assembled company in the most awful way imaginable! It was trouble enough for me to convince you to rub some vermilion onto your cheeks without you deciding to wipe pink tears now! And as for being angry, I only meant that I will pretend that I would have preferred to have kept you away from his roaming eyes. Yes, that will tantalize him! He will think you so delightfully innocent . . ."

"But I *am*—innocent, Papa!" Belinda exclaimed. "I should hope no one would ever think differently!"

Her father raised his eyes to heaven, and Kate was forced to hide her lips with her fan. In such an elegant company, surely such nonsense was out of place, or so she would have thought when

41

she was still in the country. But now she knew the picture put a polish on reality. Sir George might appear quite overpowering in the wig he reserved for evening wear, made of fox hair and white with powder applied by means of a blower, not to mention the long waistcoat covered with enbroidered peacocks, but he was in as much despair about his daughter as any father might be, no matter how humble.

At least, Kate told herself, he had had no quarrel to make with Belinda's gown, since he had ordered it himself, but she was glad of the simplicity of her own costume made of peach lustring with a fichu of ivory lace and ruffled sleeves which ended at the elbows. As for Belinda, she had been decked out by Nell, the abigail she shared with Kate, in an outfit bold enough to have excited a buzz of conversation when they had made their arrival earlier.

"Why, I declare, I feel quite naked!" Belinda had cried when she had seen herself in the pier glass after Nell was finished twisting and adjusting and had sat back on her heels, her mouth still full of pins. Pert and impertinent, Nell looked on London as high adventure and would have never returned to the country given the opportunity not to do so.

"La, miss!" she had told Kate, "only think who Miss Tigford may marry! Why, the Prince of Wales himself is still without a wife! Sir George has such high hopes for her, and so do I! There's nothing I'd like better than to be a fine lady's maid in one of them great houses on Grosvenor

42

Square and such! That's what I told Sir George himself. Such a kind gentleman he is, for he clapped me on the back and said it would all come right if we put our shoulders to the wheel, in a manner of speaking."

And now she had been given the opportunity to prove her dedication, for it had been no easy task to persuade Belinda to assume the silk polonaise gown of brilliant blue, marked with a pattern of red roses. The skirt covered a wide hoop and sported two overskirts, each shorter than the first, one a pure red and the other blue. But it was the bodice which gave Belinda most concern for it was cut very low indeed, and decorated with a red and blue bow which called attention to the bosom in what Kate considered to be a redundant manner, given the generous nature of her cousin's charms.

So horrified was Belinda by what she saw in her glass that she made no protest when Nell brushed her golden curls back over a leather pad set on the top of her head, and then used the hair iron to create a sophisticated effect heightened by a generous application of powder and the arrangement of feathers and ribbons which followed.

"There is this consolation," Kate had told her cousin. "No one will recognize you. In fact, you look very beautiful and all of twenty."

"Papa will not allow me to appear this way!" Belinda had declared, her face in flames. "This may have seemed all very well to him as an idea, but only let him see his own daughter looking like a—like a jade . . . There, I have said the word, although I know it is very wrong of me. But that is how I appear! Why, any gentleman might insult me, and I declare I could not blame him."

And although Nell protested that Sir George knew best, and Kate tried to calm her by saying that half the ladies at the ball would leave their décolletage even more uncovered, Belinda, in a rare state of outrage, had marched to her father's dressing room and demanded that his manservant give her entry.

Nell and Kate who followed close behind heard the sound of Belinda's voice rising more often than it fell until Sir George had appeared in the doorway, wearing a dressing gown and with his wig half powdered.

"You must talk some sense into her head!" He hissed. "Come, Kate. You know I cannot bear to see her excite herself so."

In the end, acting as moderator, Kate succeeded in arranging a compromise which allowed Belinda to cover more of herself with a bit of lace in return for which she submitted to an application of vermilion to her already rosy cheeks.

"Oh, whatever will they think of me?" Belinda had repeated for the hundredth time as they had stepped down from the carriage and, "Whatever will they think?" as they climbed the stairs with Sir George, like a warder, coming close behind. But, in the end, there was only a buzz when she and Kate were announced, and had Belinda been able to hear what was being said, she would have felt comforted, for most of the comments concerned the two girl's contrasting beauty, one so fair, the other with her auburn curls which she had rebelliously refused to more than sprinkle with powder.

The footman's voice was high and very clear and Kate's heart lodged in her throat for a moment when she heard Dev's name. "Four years," she whispered to herself, meaning that there was certain to be a difference in him. And then, to ward off the blow were there to be one, she closed her eyes, only to open them again when she heard her uncle chuckle.

"What do you think of him, Belinda?" he demanded. "You cannot complain that he is not handsome. And I like a fellow with a bit of swagger to him. Look at him taking the measure of the room. Oh, what a saucy chap he is and no mistake! He thinks the world his oyster, but then so did I when I was five and twenty! So did I!"

Kate stared the length of the long room at the tall, dark gentleman whose shoulders seemed to strain at the blue superfine of his jacket. His skin was bronzed to a degree as to make the gentlemen about him seem a sickly pale, and he wore no wig but rather had his dark hair pulled into a queue just below the collar. Neckcloth, cravat and wrist frills were of the whitest lawn which only served to make his skin duskier in shade.

So, she had been right, Kate thought with a wry smile. He was not the Dev she had helped onto his horse four years ago. He had been scarcely more than a boy then himself, but now he was fully a man and more handsome than he had been before. How could she have been so foolish as to think to see him appear as a fop? But he had spoken of the folly of his acquaintances . . .

And then Kate thought she understood, for the gentlemen who came behind Dev were all young like himself, and although their faces were not bronzed as his they had the same way about them. Something about how they walked the empty length of the dance floor told her that they were defiant, that no one made rules for them but themselves, and that they possessed a confidence close to arrogance.

All conversation seemed to have stopped since the moment Dev had bent over his hostess's hand. And now it resumed slowly, the most common sound to be heard being women's shrill giggles. Yes, of course, Kate told herself, staring as though hypnotized at the advancing figure, these fine gentlemen would be womanizers of the first water. They would drink but never be found too far in their cups. They would wager and win. And Dev had come back to join them.

He and his fellows had come close enough by now so that Kate thought it would be best if she were to move behind the column beside which she stood, and would have done so had she not remembered that, even if he noticed her, which was not likely, he would never associate her with the young boy who had pulled off his boot and fallen in the mud. She remembered how cheerful had had been, despite the pain, and the ribald song he had sung. She thought she had liked him

46

better then than she did now at the head of his swaggering friends.

There was a sudden confusion as the musicians mounted the platform at last and began to tune their instruments. The rim of guests standing about the dance floor seemed to dissolve as gentlemen went in search of partners. A surprising number of these ladies, meanwhile, found their way to Lord Gilcrest and his friends, and there was a great fluttering of fans and feathers and bold laughter. Dev's expression, Kate had time to notice, was sardonic.

"Now, my dear," she heard Sir George say to Belinda, "you will proceed with my little plan. I want you to parade just there before the dancing is started. It is an open space and you will be noticed."

"But why should I wish to parade alone in the middle of a ballroom?" Belinda demanded. "There is no reason for it. People will think that I am mad."

Sir George took her more tightly by the arm and his face appeared to swell like a great, ruddy balloon.

"Only listen to me!" he muttered. "Only listen to me, I implore you! You are to be looking for something, do you understand?"

"Looking for what?" Belinda cried in great bewilderment. "What would I hope to find in the center of an empty ballroom?"

"Something you are going to lose when you are standing there," Sir George said grimly. "That necklace you are wearing of blue brilliants. You will recall that was part of the outfit I chose for you. It is far from your most precious bit of jewelry, I think."

"Why, as to that," Belinda replied, "you know I have never cared for it. But still I do not understand . . ."

"You are to pass close to Lord Gilcrest," her father told her, "and you are to be fingering the necklace in a careless way. As you come beside the gentleman, give the cord which holds the brilliants a tug. I have tested it and it will break in an instant. The stones will scatter about the floor . . ."

"What!" Belinda cried. "Am I to get down on my knees and crawl about searching for them? I know you would have me go far to catch his lordship's attention, Papa. My gown is proof enough of that. But I think to crawl about on the floor is to go *too far!*"

Sir George's eyes seemed to bulge out of his face as though someone held his cravat from behind and was intent on garrotting him.

"You are bamming me, miss!" he said warningly.

"I do not think she is, Uncle," Kate warned in a low voice. "You would do well to finish your explanation quickly so that the plan can be seen in a piece."

"*You* see it already, don't you, Kate?" Sir George replied in a low voice. "Sometimes I think that I should be working hand in hand with you instead of with Belinda. But she *is* my daughter, and I owe her my best efforts. Ah, yes. Belinda! Listen, Child. You break the string of brilliants and they roll about on the floor. You do *not* crawl about. You stand and look helpless. Helpless, do you understand! I know Dev. He's a good natured sort, unlike some of those cubs he rams about with. Mind you, they'll all go down on hands and knees once they catch sight of you. But Dev is different. He would do the same if you were eighty and had cross-eyes, to boot."

"What shall I do after I thank them?" Belinda asked obediently.

"You will refuse the attentions of all of them except Dev," her father replied. "I think we may depend on him to live up to my expectations. If he does not, it will be the first time he has passed up an opportunity to meet a pretty girl."

Five

Belinda's entry onto the dance floor was not as graceful as her father might have wished, but since he was at fault by virtue of having pushed her, Kate did not think he would dare cast blame later. It was also true that Belinda's casual stroll—"as though you were meeting friends on the other side of the room," Sir George had muttered just before propelling her forward—consisted of a troubled advance of the sort to indicate that enemy guns were just ahead. But she was graceful. And long before she had reached the spot appointed for the deed to be done, all of Lord Gilcrest's gentleman friends were staring at her with open admiration, despite the fact that the ladies who had joined them were making open blandishments of their charms.

As for Lord Gilcrest himself, he was sufficiently distracted by the importuning of a young lady who kept tugging at his arm that he did not look around until one of his friends muttered something to him, and he turned. Kate tried to see her cousin through his eyes and felt her cheeks grown warm. Belinda had come to a halt, one hand on the necklace and there was such a contrast between the innocence of her and the flamboyant way in which she was decked out that the result was a voluptuous effect which Kate thought must strike everyone who looked at her.

And, indeed, even the chattering ladies grew silent. It was a strange moment as though, Kate thought, this was some strange, savage ceremony and Belinda was the maiden who was to be sacrificed. She wished that was not so close to being the case exactly.

Belinda pulled the strand of brilliants and they broke. Kate heard her uncle draw in a satisfied breath as the stones scattered about the floor. Instantly Lord Gilcrest's friends were after them and the young ladies were gathering their skirts as close around them as the hoops would allow and making little screams as though a mouse was loose. A crowd gathered from elsewhere in the ballroom to see what had happened and there was a general uproar. In the center of it all Belinda stood quite still, her hand still at her throat, and she was very pale.

Because the gathering of the brilliants was a game of sorts the gentlemen were soon uproarious. One of their number announced, to the general merriment, that he meant to demand a kiss for every brilliant that he returned to its owner. And another dashing rogue tried to take his reward on the finding of a single stone by clasping Belinda about the waist and then darting away before she could make a protest.

"Uncle!" Kate cried. "You are not going to allow such impertinence, surely! You will not stand here and allow your own daughter to be publicly humiliated!"

"My dear Kate," Sir George replied ponderously, "you are too fresh from the country to understand the ways of Society. Certainly they are teasing her, and so they should, being red-blooded young gentlemen as I was once. But it is teasing, nothing more. A pretty girl with a cachet must expect such things."

"Belinda's cachet, as you call it, is her innocence," Kate declared angrily. "Now you and everyone else here may know that she is not being humiliated, but I am certain that Belinda does not know it. See how scarlet she is! She does not dare to move, poor thing!"

"Ah, but Dev has noticed her," Sir George replied, placing one finger beside his nose. "See. He is searching for the brilliants, too. And, if the silly gel can remember what I told her, she will give him a very special thanks when he returns what he has gathered. A very special thanks indeed!"

Kate looked across the room and found that the scramble for brilliants had become even more uproarious, with the young gentlemen taking advantage of their having to bend and kneel by managing to touch an ankle here and there, which resulted in a great deal of commotion on the part of the ladies, none of them however being disconcerted enough to go elsewhere. In the midst of all the confusion Belinda stood like a statue, clearly quite terrified.

"You see how Dev is looking at her?" Sir George demanded. "Oh, he has an eye for the ladies, has Dev! Look! He is going to join the others in gathering up the stones! Damme, he'll make a skylark when he finds out that Belinda belongs to me."

"If she belongs to you, Uncle," Kate said furiously, "then you should be taking better care of her than this. I do not want to be rude, sir. Indeed, I have such a deal to thank you for that I have hesitated to speak a word. But now I must speak out. You may send me back to the country in disgrace. I do not care. But you must know that what you are doing to my cousin is an absolute disgrace, and anyone with a bit of sense would tell you that, straight out. I can only wonder that Lady Prudence did not speak out. But since she did not, I must."

"Dash it, Child," Sir George replied, brushing her protests away as casually as though her words were flies, "you're nothing but a bundle of nerves tonight. Now, will you admit that I am a man of the world . . ."

Kate saw that further truth-telling would be useless. "Of course you are, sir," she replied, looking intently at the floor.

"And do you know me for a loving father?"

"Of course you love your daughter, sir," Kate retorted, "but that is not precisely the point . . ."

"You think that because she is the center of attention, she has been humiliated," her uncle continued, frowning until the bushy eyebrows came together. "But that is not the case at all. She has been noticed. There is nothing more to it than that. From now on she will be the girl who broke her chain of brilliants and made Dev's friends scramble for them. Such a story will be the making of her. And then, of course, she will have met Dev. That is the important thing, eh?"

He was so self-confident in his long silk coat with the broad velvet cuffs, so full of himself in the embroidered waistcoat which nearly came to his knees, so certain that nothing he could do was wrong as he postured in such a way that everyone could see the turn of his calf set off in their white silk stockings, that had the matter not been so serious Kate might have laughed. Instead she took his arm.

"All that you say is no doubt correct, Uncle," she said, making use of her most winning smile in her attempt to coax him, "but is it worth the torment that Belinda is going through? Only look at her face! How can you bear it, sir?"

"Why, if a moment's discomfort will win her a reputation and perhaps a fine, spanking husband to boot, then I can stand it very well," Sir George replied. "The ladies always have something to bother them. The vapors there, hysterics here, a flood of tears! If gentlemen were to take them as seriously as they take themselves, we would all find ourselves in a pretty pickle, I declare."

Kate felt a fury build inside her, not so much against her uncle as in opposition to a society which would make the values he had just expressed acceptable. And it was true. He did not think that he was being cruel. Belinda was a child to him and always would be, just as all the women he had ever known had been children in the sense that they must not be taken seriously. Oh, they could use their charming wiles and scheme and plot, but that kept them amused which was justification enough.

"I think you have made a great mistake," she declared. "And I intend to give my cousin what comfort I can by going to join her."

"Dash it, Kate, don't interfere!" Sir George protested. "Why, damme, you don't think I'd let any real harm come to the child!"

"She needs someone beside her now," Kate said, raising her chin defiantly and taking two steps toward her cousin. "It would be even better if you would come with me and put an end to this charade."

"Leave your cousin alone," Sir George said firmly, making as though to follow her, one arm outstretched. "Damme, Kate, don't interfere, I say!"

In her haste to keep out of her uncle's grasp, Kate did not look too carefully at where she was going, keeping her eyes trained instead on Belinda who was surrounded by admirers now, one of whom was laughing and making apparent threats to drop the brilliants he had retrieved into her bodice. As a consequence of the distress she felt for her cousin, Kate scarcely looked down when she stumbled over something and would have continued on her way, no doubt, had someone not addressed her.

"Pardon me, my dear young lady," a gentleman said dryly, "but you seem to be standing on my hand."

Kate knew who had spoken before she looked down. Dev was kneeling on the floor with several brilliants in his hand and, as she looked down at him, it was so much like the first time they had met, when he had been sprawled beside the stone wall with one foot caught in the stirrup, that it took all her self-control not to show that she recognized him. He, too, must have seen some likeness in her to the 'boy' who had come to his rescue, for as their eyes met a puzzled expression came into his.

"Strange," he murmured, rising and making a bow. "You must forgive me, but you seem so familiar to me and yet I cannot think where we have met. I do not think I could have forgotten you, and yet . . ."

"I am sorry that I was not more careful where I was going," Kate said quickly. "Certainly I did not mean to step on you."

But she could not distract him so easily. His eyes were tracing her face now and he was deep in thought. Kate found that she was tense with the fear that it might come to him where they had met before.

"I could not have seen you at an entertainment such as this," he mused, "because this is the first such I have attended in this country for four years, and four years ago you would have been too young . . ."

He paused then and Kate held her breath.

"The memory is on the top of my mind," she heard him mutter. "It was not that I simply saw you. We spoke. I will recognize your voice when I hear it."

"I am afraid you have confused me with someone else, sir," Kate said as crisply as she could manage.

"Impossible," he said bluntly, rising so that now he was looking down at her. His dark eyes were so intense that Kate had to resist the impulse to shiver. She started to pass him but he put out his hand.

"The strange thing is that I have no memory of the hair," he went on. "And yet how can that be? That shade of red is so extraordinary . . . You do well not to powder it too thick, Miss . . ."

Kate ignored the hint. "You must excuse me, sir," she said, "but I have business elsewhere."

He had not touched her with that outstretched hand, but she was afraid he might. Certainly if he was as wild as his friends there was no limit to which he might go to restrain her.

"What an extraordinary person you are," he said boldly. "It has been my experience that beautiful young ladies do not conduct business at a

58

ball. Or, if they do, they do not call it by that name."

But Kate ignored the remark, for at the moment it was made she saw that the gentleman who had threatened to demand a kiss for each of the brilliants he recovered was repeating his warning as he approached Belinda. As for his companions, they laughed and clapped their hands with considerable enthusiasm, while the young ladies made a great pretense of being shocked.

"I trust you will not attempt to detain me, sir," Kate said tartly.

He bowed at that and grinned. "It would be kind of you to let me be your close observer for a few moments more until the memory of when and where we met comes back to me," he said. "Surely there is no pressing reason . . ."

"Your fine friends provide a pressing reason, sir," Kate said angrily. "I wonder you can stand aside and let them make a mockery of my cousin as they are doing."

"Your cousin?" the young marquess said, turning to stare at Belinda. "Ah! So that is what you are in a stew about."

"Consider, sir," Kate retorted. "If she were your sister, would you allow this to happen?"

Dev's smile faded. "Why, you are really outraged, aren't you?" he demanded. "But they mean nothing by it. And if your cousin does not like their manner she can retire."

"Leaving her brilliants behind her, I suppose," Kate snapped. "I see no reason why she should be forced to do anything of the sort."

"Most young ladies," he began with a frown, "would enjoy the attention your cousin is receiving. Indeed, you take a good deal on yourself to imply that that is not the case."

"Only look at her!" Kate demanded. "You do not have to be a student of human nature to know that she is terrified. I assure you, she is not pretending to be shy. None of this ever would have happened if her father had not pressed her into it!"

Kate stopped as soon as the words were spoken and covered her lips with her fingertips. But, of course, it was too late. And then, because Belinda was being forced to twist her head now to keep from being kissed, she became quite reckless.

"He wanted her to attract your attention, sir," she continued, "and until he has evidence that she has done so, he will do nothing to help her! Now, let me pass at once!"

"Well, if that is the way of it . . ." Kate heard him mutter. And then he turned and strode to where Belinda stood. In disbelief Kate saw him motion away the young gentleman who had demanded kisses, and then, a smile replacing a scowl, he made a formal bow to Belinda. Kate was too far away to hear what was being said, but she saw the relief on her cousin's face, and soon she seemed quite at her ease, opening her beaded reticule and holding it out for the brilliants to be put inside.

Slowly the crowd dispersed and a cotillion line began to form as the violinist raised his instrument to his chin. Some of Dev's friends chose partners from the young ladies who had joined them and others went off to one of the side rooms reserved for whist. Kate waited where she was, expecting Dev to take his leave of Belinda but, instead, her cousin's lovely face wreathed in smiles, she and the young marquess went to join the cotillion line.

Six

"You know that I am as sorry about it as you are, Fitz," Lady Prudence said as she descended from the carriage in a businesslike fashion, "but you know Sir George's feelings. I would not have let you come with me this far if I had not been certain that he would be at his club at this hour. There is no question of you coming inside the house. Be a good lad and wait here in the phaeton for me. If it will help to entertain you, you may chat with Herbert. Yes, that should be very pleasant for you both."

Lady Prudence was an admirable mother despite the fact that she saw no need to treat her four grown sons differently now than she had when they were ten. She did not so much hold conversations with them as she delivered a series of directives. The elder, Frederick, often referred to her as 'mon Generalissimo' when she was not within hearing, but it was well known that Frederick had never taken life as seriously as it deserved to be taken.

Fitz, on the other hand, took life very seriously indeed. He was a good enough looking fellow with fair hair and a pleasant face with fortunately few physical signs that he was a Mancer on his father's side. Indeed, the only drawback in his appearance was his tendency to look so extraordinarily solemn that one's spirits were inclined to plunge at the very sight of him. It was Fitz's philosophy, no doubt understandable in one possessing such a mother, that it was best to anticipate the worst to avoid unpleasant surprises. Indeed, when Lady Prudence had come to him with the news that Sir George desired that he would not continue his pursuit of Belinda, Fitz's first comment had been that he wondered why he had not been banished before.

At the same time, he was willing to let his mother make his plans for him even though he found her aggressive optimism somewhat offputting. Today, in fact, when she had proposed that he accompany her on a shopping trip which, if it could be arranged, would include Belinda too, he had willingly agreed, although continuing to frown and make disheartened comments about the unlikely future of any romance he might embark on.

Now, as his mother paraded up to the front door of Sir George's rented London residence, Fitz shielded his eyes against the sun and looked from one window to the next, hoping no doubt that Belinda would see him or that he would catch a glimpse of her, although the expression on his face made it quite clear that he thought either possibility extremely unlikely. As a matter of fact, since Belinda and Kate were in Kate's bedchamber at the back of the house, his pessimism was quite appropriate.

The two girls had been deep in conversation since escaping Sir George after breakfast that morning. Indeed, he had been so exhilarated by the success of his fine scheme the night before that he had been quite impossible. Nothing would please him but that he must run over the sequence of events again and again, and to make it worse, each time the story was told, he must pause to congratulate himself on his astuteness, rubbing his hands and in many other ways making himself so objectionable to both daughter and niece that when he proposed to disclose his plans for Belinda's next foray, both girls made claims to megrims and hurried away upstairs where they gave distinct orders to Nell that Sir George was not to be allowed into the room.

Then, settling themselves comfortably on either side of the fire with Nell sitting on a footstool between them, her mobcapped head turning back and forth as Kate answered Belinda and Belinda answered Kate, they had discussed the evening before in all its fascinating detail.

"But why won't Papa understand that Lord Gilcrest was only being kind?" Belinda said now.

Kate shook her head for they had come full

65

circle without stumbling on any answer to that particular problem. She had said nothing to her cousin of what she had blurted out to Dev thinking that that would be to humiliate her even more. But now she wondered if she should tell the truth. The secrets seemed to be piling up, although she could not think it was important for anyone except herself to know that she had met the young marquess before.

Certainly he had acted like a gentleman after he had seen that Belinda was a victim, of sorts. Kate knew she could not blame him for having misunderstood at first, since it was clear that he and his friends were accustomed to the antics of far more sophisticated young ladies. And nothing could have been more calculated to save the situation than the way he had treated Belinda throughout the remainder of the evening, even when he realized that Sir George was her father, a fact which must have given him some pause considering what Kate had let slip to him.

As for Kate herself, she had watched the developments of the evening from a safe distance, taking care to accept the dancing offers of every gentleman who had presented himself. Indeed, she had had so many partners that she could not remember all their faces now, in part because she had been so much absorbed by her cousin's little drama. Indeed, what she remembered best of the entire evening was the happy smile on Belinda's face as she had been passed down the line of the first cotillion, and her expression of rapt attention as Dev had talked intimately to her over the light collation of crimped salmon and other delicacies with which the evening had ended. Her own partner at supper, Sir Arthur Vaux, had been an amusing enough companion, but Kate had not been able to keep her full mind on the conversation, so intent was she on watching Belinda and Dev and wondering if her cousin found him as fascinating as she appeared to do.

There had been no opportunity for conversation the night before, at least not between the two girls. All the way home in the carriage Sir George had gone on and on about the success of his plan, with the effect that both Kate and Belinda were so exhausted that they both went to bed directly. But now Kate knew that, although Belinda's evening had truly been salvaged for her and she had found her companion charming, nothing was further from her mind than to continue with attempts to arouse his interest.

"I know it must have appeared to everyone that he was—well, that he was enchanted with me," her cousin had confided. "But he was only doing his best to put me at my ease. He apologized for his friends quite nicely, and over supper he had the most interesting stories to tell about Virginia. But he treated me more like a sister than anything."

Kate had scarcely dared to ask if this was any disappointment, but before she had found the words, Belinda had declared that nothing could sway her from her fondness for Fitz.

"I know Papa will think me a great fool," she said, with Nell hanging on every word, "but I know what my heart tells me. Fitz may have no fortune or a title, and no doubt he is not as charming as Lord Gilcrest for he *does* fret and worry so, but it makes me happy to be with him. Oh, Kate, do you think Papa will insist on keeping us apart when he knows just how I feel?"

That was the question Kate did not know the answer to, and she did not care to raise hopes which might be false. There were her own emotions to consider, as well, much as she might tell herself that her fascination with Dev was based on a girl's impressions and nothing more.

"Well, it is all that exciting!" Nell exclaimed suddenly. "And you are making all this bother, miss, when you could up and marry a marquess for the asking."

"It would not be for the asking, Nell," Belinda said gently. "It would mean that I would have to pretend to be someone beside myself. That is the whole point of my father's plan, don't you see?"

"But from what you've said, miss," Nell protested, "—and I've been listening that close—it seems his lordship liked you well enough for yourself."

"Well, if he liked me it was not in the way Papa has in mind," Belinda declared. "You agree, Kate, surely."

"How can I say when I have only your word for it?" Kate protested.

Belinda rose and went to look at herself in the pier glass. In her blue muslin morning gown with a demure fichu pulled across her bodice, she looked very little like the picture she had presented the night before, and, to Kate's mind, at least, infinitely more charming.

"But you saw the sort of young ladies he and his friends have to do with," Belinda cried, picking up her brush and attacking her golden curls so violently you might have thought she wished to straighten them. "Why, they are the sort of witty, artful, frivolous types which Lord Gilcrest prefers."

"As for that," Kate said dryly, "I would have rather said that they were silly, sharp-tongued and presumptuous."

"But certainly they know how to dress in the height of fashion."

"Given the current mode, I am not certain that is any compliment," Kate replied tartly.

"Well, you must confess that none of them would have behaved as awkwardly as I did after I had broken the string of brilliants," Belinda countered. "Oh, what a fool I must have looked, to have made Lord Gilcrest sorry enough for me to have given me so much of his attention!"

"You did not look a fool," Kate declared firmly. "Indeed, your appearance was quite suitable to an occasion when gentlemen behaved like rude boys, and the ladies like a gaggle of geese. You were embarrassed and you showed it. I can see no harm in that. At least is was a faithful portrayal of how you really felt."

"But Papa said that was what I must avoid at all costs," Belinda said thoughtfully, "and I declare I think I begin to see the sense in it. Yes, I should dearly love to have poise, to be distressed by nothing."

"I believe that poise is one thing and deceit another," Kate told her. "Believe me, Cousin, you will do best to remain yourself. After all, that is the way Fitz likes you, is it not?"

And Belinda had happily agreed, quite willing to forget for a moment the unhappy situation she was in, for she was a cheerful creature and liked to avoid trouble when she could. But Kate, who prided herself on facing reality with all the pragmatism possible, had given a thought to the significance of the fact that Belinda was already willing to envy those painted creatures their poise. How long would it be, she wondered, before she would come to envy them other things, as well. And all because Sir George wanted her to play a role!

But an hour had passed since then, and they had covered the same territory again, ending with Belinda's now familiar plaint about her father. And it was at this moment that Lady Prudence came into the room, towering over them all. Nell, who had been reminded more than once by her ladyship that she was permitted to be more familiar with her mistress by half than she should be, jumped up from the footstool with a little cry, and pulling this and that from the wardrobe with apparent lack of discrimination, declared that she was off to mend Miss Belinda's things and left the room.

Alone with the two girls, the baroness lost no

time in delivering her opinion of the events of the evening past.

"I was not there, of course," she said, pulling off her gloves. "I thought to conciliate your papa, my dear, by keeping myself and Fitz well away. But Lucy Mattigan was there and, she thought it best to keep me well informed. Ah, you poor child! You poor, poor dear! What an embarrassment it must have been for you!"

Kate leaped at once to her cousin's defense. If nothing else had come out of the evening it had been the calming of Belinda's fears in that regard. Indeed, thanks to the assiduousness of Dev's attention, she had come to the put matter of the broken necklace into a sensible perspective. And yet here was Lady Prudence flat-footedly prepared to conjure up the humiliation.

"But it was nothing, ma'am," Kate declared. "There was a certain amount of joking as the brilliants were gathered up. Perhaps some of the gentlemen were a little bold. But polite society makes such scenes common, if what I have observed is to be trusted. And Belinda spent the rest of the evening quite comfortably attended to."

Lady Prudence raised her eyebrows which had the effect of making her eyes appear to protude even further. Her aquiline nose seemed to arch its back.

"My dear Kate," she declared. "It was precisely the remainder of the evening which I was making reference to, for I understand that Lord Gilcrest was your cousin's constant companion and that he even took her in to supper."

"Papa was very pleased," Belinda said shyly. "But then that was because his scheme seemed to go so well. You knew, of course, what was in his mind. At least he said that he had been quite frank with you."

"Oh, he was frank," Lady Prudence declared, "if that is what one calls disclosing one's own idiocies. I refrained from telling him that he was being a great fool then because I wanted to be better prepared for an attack. And now that I know something of the famous Lord Gilcrest's past, I think that it is scandalous of your papa to have allowed you to be alone in his presence for one moment, Child, not to speak of an entire evening."

"His past?" Kate and Belinda demanded simultaneously.

"Your papa must be aware of it, or if he is not than he should be," Lady Prudence continued. "It is not the sort of thing meant for tender ears like yours, my dears. But I intend to be here when the gentleman returns from his club later this afternoon and, I assure you, I will warm his ears! So my Fitz was not good enough for his daughter, eh! Well, we shall see to that!"

And with that she announced that indeed Fitz was outside in the phaeton this very moment, and that he would be pleased to accompany them all on a shopping expedition. The necessity of purchasing some silk for a new gown for Belinda was made a pressing matter in a few seconds, and Kate saw that her cousin was eager to go.

"I believe I will remain at home," she said carefully. "I am afraid that my head aches a little."

"Oh, but we only made up our headaches to escape papa," Belinda reminded her.

"But this time mine is real," Kate declared. "I expect it is because I am tired."

That was not the reason though, and well she knew it. Was it true that scandal tarnished Dev's name in some manner, scandal of the sort not fit for her ears? Kate thought that she would not be able to rest until she knew just what it was.

Seven

Alone in the house except for the servants, Kate
gave in to the restlessness which her thoughts
induced and fell to pacing back and forth across
the sitting room, pausing now and then to look
out one of the long windows onto the street filled
with curricles, sedan chairs, old-fashioned ba-
rouches and hackney coaches—all, it seemed, employed in carrying elaborately dressed and be-
wigged members of the *haut ton* on their first
social round of the day. This was the very Society
Dev had wanted to escape four years ago. No
doubt, Kate thought, he knew its lures and temp-
tations far better than she. Indeed, if as Lady
Prudence said, there was scandal attached to his
name, she would not be surprised.

Strange, in what a new light he had appeared
to her the night before. It had, she thought, quite

changed her feeling about him to see him as the head of that swaggering group of gentlemen who clearly ruled the social roost. Possessed of vast fortunes and titles of every sort, and young and handsome to boot, they ruled over their little world. Granted that four years ago Dev had said he wanted to be rid of them, but the Virginia experiment must have changed that, for he had seemed to her at least to be quite in his element when he had led his friends into the ballroom. Granted that he had been kind to Belinda. She must not forget that. But being generous to innocent young ladies was not, she thought, an occupation which took up a great deal of his time. And it was the way he lived that must concern her if she wished to determine how best Belinda—and perhaps herself—should deal with him.

This resolve had just been made when, pausing at a window, Kate saw the object of her reflections ride up to the house on a handsome chestnut mare. She took a deep breath and held it as Dev dismounted and flung the reins to one of the ragged urchins who were always on hand close by where the gentry lived, hoping to earn a few pennies watching horses. Disturbed as she was by his sudden and unexpected appearance, Kate still did not fail to notice that the coin which passed from Dev's hand to the boy's was silver and not bronze, and she marked it as still another sign of his generosity. But there was arrogance, she thought, in the confidence with which he mounted the steps, a handsome fellow in the glistening boots and buckskin riding breeches which he wore with the same distinction that he had worn a more formal costume the night before.

But why had he come? To see her uncle? To see Belinda? Perhaps he had been as taken with her as he had pretended. Kate could not but hope that was not so, for were he to join forces with Sir George, in a sense, Belinda would never be able to resist. Kate remained by the window, well hidden by the drapes, expecting to see Dev descend the steps at any moment since neither her uncle nor her cousin were at home. But instead there was a tap at the sitting room door and the footman appeared with word that a Lord Gilcrest had called to see her.

Kate knew she should pretend not to be home. Certainly it was not entirely proper for her to entertain him alone. If she had been a married lady, of course, there would be no problem, but as it was . . . Besides, why should she wish to see him? He belonged to a world which she knew nothing of and did not care to join. But wait . . . was it not more important still for her to know why he had come and asked for her. Except for the brief moment when they had exchanged words on the dance floor, they had never met. Certainly Kate had managed things so that they had not been formally introduced. But, of course, Belinda would have given him her name if he had mentioned her cousin. Which meant that . . . oh, but she did not know what it meant and could not resist the temptation to find out. After all, she had already determined that he did not recognize her so what was the danger? But first, all must be quite respectable.

"Tell the gentleman I will be with him in ten minutes or less," she told the footman. "Let him wait in the drawing room. And then please find Nell at once and send her to my room."

As it happened it did not take much persuasion on Kate's part to convince Nell that she should don one of her gowns and allow herself to be introduced to Lord Gilcrest as a friend.

"A very silent friend," Kate impressed on her, knowing Nell's tendency to ramble into other people's conversations. "There, you look very well indeed. Blue suits you. And now I must just take a look in the glass myself . . . Remember, no one is to know."

"But what if Tom sees me decked out like this, miss?" Nell demanded, making reference to the very footman who had shown Lord Gilcrest in a few minutes before.

"You are on particularly good terms with him, I believe," Kate declared, adjusting the lace at her elbows and seeing that her full, green muslin overskirt was draped gracefully over the full white petticoat. It did not matter how she looked, of course, but it was as well to present a tidy appearance. Or so she told herself. Also in the name of neatness, she spent another minute arranging her red curls.

"I declare I hope Tom *does* see me, miss," Nell said, coming to stand behind Kate who stood aside to let the abigail see herself. "And I quite understand your meaning. If he does see, I'm to tell him that you particularly wished to see the gentleman on business or some such, and that you could not be alone with him, and to have me there as your maid would have been much the same thing as being alone, in a manner of speaking. Oh, there's no need to worry about Tom, miss, although if I were to give him a half crown it would do no harm."

Kate had put a halt to Nell's volubility with a coin rummaged from her reticule and in a few minutes they were entering the drawing room, although it was necessary to cross the hall under Tom's horrified stare to do it.

Dev was standing in the center of the pretty blue and white room with its panels and Wedgewood design and Adam fireplace, and when the ladies entered the room he came toward them at once, his dark handsome face framed by his thick black hair, the standing collar of his riding jacket and the white, lawn cravat which he had knotted simply.

"Miss Harrison," he said. "How very good of you to see me."

Remembering the language he had used on their first meeting when he had thought she was a boy and the ribald song he had sung to keep back the pain, Kate was amused. She introduced Nell by her own name as quickly as was possible, for there was a dazed expression in the little maid's eyes which indicated that she had been particular struck by the young marquess's appearance. Indeed, when he made his bow to her, she swayed to an extent that Kate thought it the better part of wisdom to hurry her to a chair.

"Miss Robinson is just up from the country for a visit," she improvised as Nell made it adequately clear that she could not drag her eyes away from him. "Everything and everybody look a bit more than life-size, I dare say."

"Was that your own experience, Miss Harrison?" Dev asked her. "I understand from your cousin that you are recently up from Kent. A lovely county, that. There was a friend I used to visit there. His family had the Fandrill estate near Canterbury. Do you know it?"

Remembering that it had been Fandrill Hall at which he had been staying when he had had the hunting accident four years ago, Kate felt herself go quite cold. He had recognized her then! That was the reason he had come here, to remind her of it, to humiliate her by playing cat and mouse as his friends had with Belinda the night before. Well then, he should see from the start that she was not prepared to put up with it! The temper which her father said had come with the hair began to flame.

"Yes, indeed, sir," she said sharply, "I do know Fandrill Hall. Is there any particular point you would like to make about it? If there is, I wish you would proceed at once!"

"La!" she heard Nell cry, no doubt because in her world below stairs a casual comment such as that his lordship had made did not receive such a severe reception. Indeed, Kate though she could see from the expression on Dev's face that he had no inkling of what had so enraged her. Instantly she felt the fool and told herself that was bound to be the way of it. Last night she had blurted out something of a confidential nature which he must have thought quite odd, and today, within a few minutes of meeting him again, she had near as well bitten off his head for having made a casual comment about someone he knew in Kent. What better proof did she need that he lived in such a different worlds that she must be gauche whenever she made an intrusion into his?

"I confess I did not come here to discuss Fandrill Hall with you, Miss Harrison," the young marquess replied. "Certainly I would never have mentioned the spot had I imagined that it would set you off in such a manner. But then, perhaps, if you know young Felix Fandrill that might easily be explained."

Kate drew herself up. "I do not know Mr. Fandrill," she replied, "but if I did, I do not know what business it would be of yours, sir."

Dev smiled that slow, roguish smile which Kate remembered far too well. "Well in that, at least, Miss Harrison, I think that we agree," he said. "Will you permit me to add that your temper does not seem to have improved since our brief conversation last night?"

"That is a very personal comment, sir, and one I do not care to respond to," Kate replied coolly. "Since we have covered the reasons why you are *not* here, perhaps we may proceed to why you are."

"Very concisely put," he told her. "I think from Miss Robinson's expression that she agrees."

"La, sir!" Nell exclaimed. "I don't agree to nothing."

Kate shot her a warning glance and Dev, after a startled pause apparently decided to ignore such an enigmatic, not to mention ungrammatical, comment. And grateful for his forbearance, Kate invited him to sit down, taking her own seat on the sofa beside the abigail who continued to look back and forth from her to her guest with eyes which threatened to pop.

"I must begin by making a confession," Dev said with that ease of manner which never seemed to desert him. "As you know, perhaps, your uncle is an acquaintance of mine, and I am well aware of his habit of spending this particular time of day at his club. And it is also true that I determined to come here not more than half an hour ago, when I observed your cousin and an older lady proceeding down Piccadilly in a carriage. I was eager, you see, to speak to you in private."

And with that he turned his dark eyes on Nell who broke into a nervous giggle and gave evidences of being ready to rush from the room.

"Miss Robinson is the soul of discretion, sir," Kate said grimly, reaching out to grip the abigail's arm in the event her message was not clear. "Besides, it is my wish that she remain."

"I bow to your wishes, Miss Harrison," Dev replied, inclining his head. "Always your faithful servant and so on."

"And now perhaps we may come to the purpose

of your visit, Lord Gilcrest," Kate said stiffly. "I confess to being confused as to what you could possibly have to say to me of such a confidential nature that it was necessary for you to plot the whereabouts of every other member of this household before coming here."

Again he inclined his head as though admitting to a defeat, but at the same time Kate saw that he was smiling. The thought that anything about the situation might amuse him infuriated her.

"Surely it would be only natural for me to want to make apologies for my light-hearted friends," he said. "I sent a note off to each of them this morning making a point of the fact that they caused Miss Tigford genuine embarrassment."

Kate stared at him intently. "Why, I do not believe it!" she exclaimed. "No, my good sir, you would never do such a thing. I am certain of it!"

"Ah ha!" Dev cried. "I thought I was right about you. Not only have you a temper, but you understand people very well indeed. You are right, Miss Harrison. I sent no notes. If I had done so, my friends would have thought I had gone mad. That is because they know me well. But how it was you managed to guess . . ."

"If I had believed you, would you have let me remain deceived?" Kate demanded.

"No doubt I would have done," the young marquess told her. "It would not have mattered what I did since that would have terminated the conversation."

So engrossed had Nell become in the conversation that she had leaned her elbow on her knee and propped her chin in both hands in a manner more befitting a place around the kitchen table than the sofa in the drawing room.

"Terminated?" Kate heard her murmur now. "Peculiar word, that."

"Really, sir," Kate retorted. "You puzzle me exceedingly. You mean to say that you came here prepared to lie to me for the purpose of discovering whether or not I was capable of seeing that lie for what it was. In the case of my not being sufficiently astute, you intended to take your leave. Have I put it correctly? For if I have I think I have my own questions as to your degree of sanity."

Dev continued to smile. Nothing she could say, apparently, could disturb him.

"You have it right in essence, Miss Harrison," he said. "I did not come here with a particular ploy in mind, but that is by-the-by. The important thing is that I needed to determine something more about you. To know you better in the shortest time possible was my aim."

"And have you accomplished it, sir?" Kate demanded stiffly. "Or are there other tests you care to administer before you disclose your mysterious purpose in coming here. Perhaps I could ask a few friends to write character references for me."

Dev pretended to be occupied with straightening his white lawn cuffs and Kate could tell from the tight twist of his mouth that he was trying hard to keep himself from laughing aloud. Clearly her irony amused him, but something about him made it impossible for her to speak in any other way. Indeed she had never met anyone who had such a curious effect on her. It was outrageous, of course, for him to suggest that he had to be certain of her character before they continued to talk, and she would have been quite justified to have left the room with Nell in tow. But something kept her listening to him, something more than simple curiosity.

"Last night when you stepped on my hand . . ." Dev began.

"La, miss, you didn't never do such a thing!" Nell exclaimed. "Step on the gentleman's hand, indeed!"

"Your friend has a strange way of addressing you, Miss Harrison," Dev said, smiling his slow smile. "But I think I understand. Yes, Miss Robinson, she *did* step on my hand and, if you will permit me, I will explain the reason for our peculiar introduction to one another at another time. But the fact is that we did meet, Miss Harrison, and you did say something to me concerning your friend Miss Tigford which interested me exceedingly."

Kate lowered her eyes and stared at her clenched hands. Was it possible that he was worried about the very same aspect of the affair which concerned her so much? He had called her an astute judge of human nature, but she thought he must be more discerning by far if he was about to say what she anticipated him to.

"It was a relatively simple matter to keep things in hand last night," he told her, quite serious now. "Your cousin was not seriously embarrassed in the end. But, if your uncle is up to the trick I think, things will become more and more awkward for Miss Tigford. And she is such a charming, natural soul I would not like to see that happen. And so I think it comes to this. I know from what you said last night that you want to help your cousin. Will you, perhaps, allow me to assist?"

Eight

It was Lady Prudence's misfortune that Sir George chose to return from his club so early that, when Harry proudly drove her and Fitz and Belinda up to the house, he was just about to go in at the door. Kate, who had only just had time to help Nell out of her gown and back into her own, all the while murmuring admonitions to the abigail to reveal nothing of what she had overheard, heard the carriage pull up to the front. "Oh dear!" she murmured as she looked out the window of her chamber and saw her uncle throw back his shoulders until the embroidered gray satin of his coat strained at the seams. "Oh dear!" she said again as he went marching back down the steps to meet the carriage at the curb.

"Lady Prudence," Sir George said, making a deep bow, his face expressionless as he swept his feathered, three-cornered hat from his head. "An unexpected pleasure. And I see your youngest son is with you. Good day, sir. Shall I say that seeing you is simply unexpected?"

"There's no call to browbeat Fitz," Lady Prudence said protectively, taking Sir George's hand as she descended from the carriage. "It was my notion to go out shopping, and I saw no reason why Fitz should not go along. He is such a help when it comes to carrying things, you know."

"You spoke of reasons, ma'am," Sir George said in an outraged voice. "I think the presence of my daughter was quite reason enough to give you pause. If you care to take your son shopping with you, that is your affair. If you take Belinda, it is mine."

"Oh, what a great deal of gammon you talk, sir!" Lady Prudence said with a shrug of her shoulders, starting toward the house, the billowing hoopskirt of her walking gown forcing Sir George to stand aside. "Belinda, mind you bring that small package of gloves with you. You may wait, Fitz, since Sir George is not gracious enough to allow you inside. Talk to Harry. It will help to pass the time."

"I do not want your son sitting outside my house, ma'am!" Sir George stormed, slapping one pantalooned leg smartly.

"Fitz is not a disease, sir!" Lady Prudence replied, tapping Sir George smartly on the shoulder from her elevated position on the second step. "I will not have you speak of him as though he were!"

"Damme, ma'am!" Sir George sputtered. "You have done me sufficient favors so that I have no wish to appear ungrateful, but I think you know enough of my plans for Belinda's future to understand that it will not do to have your son advertise his presence here so!"

Lady Prudence tapped him on the other shoulder. "Since I intend to have a word with you, sir," she replied, "and since I expect Harry to be waiting here with the carriage when I am through, and since there is not time for him to take Fitz home and return here before I will require him . . ."

"Oh, very well!" Sir George roared. "Very well! You will always have your way, won't you? It's no great wonder to me that your husband is particular about remaining in the country, I declare. Why, I hate to think of the merry dance you lead the poor chappy. Tell your son to come into the house. But it is to be the last time and Belinda is to go directly upstairs for I will not countenance any conversation between them."

"Never mind, my dear," Lady Prudence consoled Belinda as she paused at the top of the stairs to wait for the girl. "It is not your fault if your papa prefers to act like a brute!"

"A brute!" Sir George cried, his face as scarlet as the inserts in his waistcoat. "Damme, you've no right to say that, ma'am, no right at all! You know the reason I prefer to make this effort. It is for the gel's good."

Lady Prudence raised her fan to the side of her mouth. "Ah, and as for that, I think I will soon persuade you that you have been mistaken," she said. "Come along, Fitz. How many times have I told you not to lag so? And you, Harry. Stop grinning like an idiot, if you please. Dear me! I see we have attracted rather a large crowd, Sir George. Perhaps we should go inside directly. Yes. Just so. Now, up the stairs, Belinda. It will be the last time you will have to hide from my son, I think. And Fitz, there is the drawing room. You and I will talk in the library, I think, Sir George, since it is to be a serious conversation."

And with that she was gone, although Sir George lingered for a moment until he had seen his daughter safely up the stairs and young Fitz in the drawing room with the door closed behind him.

"I wonder what she intends to tell him?" Kate mused aloud, when Belinda had recounted what had happened to her friend who had only seen the dumb show of it, not having dared to raise the window.

"She seems to think that it is something which will make a change," Belinda said wistfully, "but I cannot think what sort of change she means. Oh, Kate! Fitz was so attentive while we were shopping. But, of course, he has the dismals. Fancy, Papa trying to keep him from seeing me! It is all so terribly unfair. Dear Fitz, I cannot bear to think of him sitting all alone in the drawing room. I mean to say, we are only separated by a floor and yet he might as well be a million miles away."

Because of what had passed between herself and Dev, Kate had determined that she would say nothing of Lord Gilcrest's visit. She had been fretting over the arrangement they had come to just before her cousin's return, but now, seeing the genuine sadness in her blue eyes, she decided that she had been right to take part in the plan. Knowing Fitz it was difficult to understand what Belinda could possibly see in him to admire, but that was her affair and if her affections led her in that direction then, in Kate's opinion, she must be allowed to follow.

"Lady Prudence was so sweet," Belinda went on, taking off her bonnet. "I declare, she even went so far as to hold long conversation with the boy who drives their carriage, and in a very loud voice indeed, to make it possible for Fitz and I to have a little tête-à-tête. Of course, when we were going down Piccadilly where it is so very crowded, she was a good deal stared at. But that never seems to trouble her, although Fitz will complain about it. He never dares to speak straight out to her, you know. It is the same with Frederick, Frank and Fairbanks. And although I thought it strange when I first met them, I have changed my mind. She is the sort of woman who often knows best, and it follows that she must be given her head."

Since it was usual that some time spent with Fitz had this effect on Belinda, making her unusually voluble and inclined to philosophizing, Kate made no particular note of what was being said. Indeed, while her cousin continued her monologue—first in front of the wardrobe where she put away her pelisse and walking shoes and then before the mirror where she proceeded to brush her hair—Kate gave herself up to thought about what had occurred between her and Dev.

He had, she must admit, behaved admirably, although it had taken her some time to overcome her distrust. Perhaps, if she had encountered him with only the strength of their first meeting to influence her, she would not have been so wary of him. But having seen him enter the ballroom—so smart, so self-assured with that arrogant, handsome group of gentlemen-about-the-town whom he chose to make his friends—had given her pause. Perhaps, Kate thought now, he was one person when he was with them, and quite another when apart. But in that case would she ever know who he really was?

Kate told herself that was beside the point. She and Dev had nothing in common except a desire to help Belinda out of her present difficulties. And when he had first disclosed the purpose of his visit to her, Kate had not believed that even that could bring them to terms.

He had begun by reminding her of what she had said when they had met the evening before, and at first Kate had pretended not to remember.

"But what could my uncle have had to do with my cousin having accidentally broken a string of brilliants?" she had retorted. "I am afraid, sir, that you must have misunderstood me. After all, your friends were making a good deal of racket and . . ."

"I heard precisely what you said, Miss Harrison," he told her, his eyes insistent. "You said that your cousin's papa had forced her into it, and I cannot think of anything else which would apply except the breaking of the necklace. Indeed, you went further and mentioned something about attracting my attention. I confess it was such a puzzling remark that I might well have forgotten it, had I not soon discovered that Sir George is the papa in question."

Kate averted her eyes. "I cannot think why the identity of my cousin's father would have any bearing on anything, sir," she hedged.

"Why, there is this!" Dev declared, jumping to his feet and coming to stand beside the sofa as though to make his point all the more forceful. "I have known Sir George since I was a boy. Not in the country, you understand, since my estate is in Devon, but here in town. Indeed, I learned to play faro by watching him and deep basset, too, for that matter. And now, it seems, he is making himself expert in another game, and that I seem to be playing opposite him. Come, Miss Harrison, is not that the way of it?"

On the one hand it delighted Kate that he had put the pieces of the puzzle together so cleverly, but on the other hand this placed her in a very awkward situation.

"He's waiting for his answer, miss," she heard Nell whisper. "Say something, do."

This time Kate had not tried to hush her, since she thought it quite probable that Nell's previous gaffe had been sufficient to have allowed Dev to guess Miss Robinson's real station in the household. Besides, she could not think of two things at once, and what he had just said demanded her complete attention.

"I think," she said carefully, "that if you suspect my uncle of something, you should go to him directly and make your accusation."

"I think you should have been a diplomat, Miss Harrison," the young marquess had replied. "But if I went to Sir George, he would deny everything and nothing would be accomplished. My other options are no more promising, I think. Perhaps you might be put in a more accommodating frame of mind if you were to hear them. Or perhaps you have already thought it out for yourself."

At that point Kate had been forced to confess that she had not. And, although she did not add it, she had been too engrossed in Belinda's plight, not to mention her own feelings, to consider what was happening from his viewpoint. But having come this far—and, she realized, by admitting that he had options she had in a way confessed that his guess about Sir George's plans had been correct—she decided that she might as well go on, although where all this was leading them she was not certain.

"Consider this, then, if you will," Dev had told her. "Although first, perhaps, I should make my position clear. Your cousin is a charming young lady, as well as being sensitive and delicate, I think. If that were not the case I should not be so troubled. But, as it is, she must be the main consideration. And I cannot in good conscience pretend that she and I could ever be anything but friends."

Kate nodded her head quickly to indicate that he need not go on, that she understood. It was just as she had thought, then. Like his friends Dev was not interested in ladies who fell outside the circle of sophisticates with whom he surrounded himself. Belinda might have been dressed as daringly as they the evening before, but it could not have taken more than two minutes of conversation with her for Dev to discover that she was as unlike them as night from day. It was kind of him to even go so far as to indicate that he and Belinda might be friends, she thought, since it was apparent that he chose his friends from quite a different quarter.

"I have made myself clear, then," Dev said in a low voice.

"Poor Miss Tigford," Nell was heard to mourn. "And her papa with such high hopes."

"Are you quite certain that Miss Robinson will be discreet?" Dev murmured.

"I believe that I can guarantee it, sir," Kate replied absently. "Besides, she has heard this much. She may as well hear more. Not that I am certain that either one of us should be listening to you."

"You must believe that I have nothing more than your cousin's welfare at heart," he pressed her, going to stand by the mantelpiece. How careless a thing he made elegance look, Kate thought, with the perfect flow of his cravat and the cut of his blue jacket. Why should a gentleman like himself give more than a second thought to country girls like herself and Belinda? The Dev she

95

remembered singing boisterous songs to keep away the pain of his ankle was someone quite different, and she would do well to remember it.

"I do believe it," she said in an even voice. "And now, sir, your options. Let us consider them."

It was a simple matter in the end. If he were to make it clear that he wished to be Belinda's friend and nothing more, Sir George would arrange even more outrageous ploys than that of the necklace to make him change his mind.

"He does not give up a game until every card is spent," Dev said reflectively. "In this case his daughter's charms make up the deck he plays with, I think."

Kate agreed that she did not think her uncle would give the game up easily.

"I feel disloyal talking to you like this," she confessed. "But simply to think of what might occur to him to have Belinda do convinces me that something must be done. She will not defy him, you see. She is too good-natured for that, too obedient by far."

Dev looked at her with interest. "You have considered encouraging her to rebel," he said quickly. "Do not deny it, Miss Harrison. I see it in your face. You would never comply with such a plan, I think."

"I should not take credit for a situation which will never arise," Kate protested. "My father has never forced me to do anything. Certainly he would let me choose my own husband."

"You have been very independent, then?" he ~s asked her curiously. At once Kate remembered the hoyden of a girl she had been, riding without a sidesaddle in a boy's clothing. She must divert him from this tack at once, or he might remember why her face seemed so familiar.

"We are speaking of Belinda," Kate reminded him. "Or, rather, Miss Tigford. I agree that it would be worse than useless to attempt to show my uncle that the cause he has embraced is hopeless. Perhaps he may be persuaded sometime, but not at once. But what other course is there?"

"I could make a pretense of having been captured, I suppose," Dev told her. As he leaned against the mantel, one elbow on it and his feet in their glittering leather boots crossed casually, he looked so much at ease, Kate thought, that this could just as well have been his home and not Sir George's. She wondered what would happen if her uncle should return and find Dev there. Doubtless he would place his own interpretation on it, and with his incurable optimism, assume that his friend was waiting for Belinda and that Kate had chosen to entertain him. Nell's presence, however, in his niece's gown would give him pause.

"But I do not like that solution," Dev went on. "It would only lead to other complications."

"You have your own life to consider," Kate said in a low voice.

"It is not that," he told her. "I have no obligations. Certainly I am not already affianced, although it would have made this a simpler matter had I been. But it would mean a misrepresentation to your cousin, and . . ."

"You need not fear that she would become impassioned with you," Kate assured him. "Her heart is set elsewhere."

"Then why does not her father let her follow it?" the young marquess demanded. "I suppose there are the usual reasons. Sometimes I think that no one marries for love any longer in this society."

The words were spoken with so much vehemence that Kate stared at him curiously. But before he could continue—if, indeed, he meant to—Nell had leaped to her feet, tugging the mobcap Kate had lent her down over her light brown hair and in general showing some excitement.

"I think I have a notion of how it could be done!" she said. "Is it all right if I speak, miss? I mean the damage has been done, hasn't it? It was no use for me to pretend to be a lady, in any case."

"You have not pretended to be anything you are not, Miss Robinson," Dev said with a bow. "Indeed, I wish that more of the ladies I knew were as delightfully fresh as you. By all means speak your mind."

At the compliment he paid her, Nell turned a bright red but she was not too disconcerted to proceed. "What if it was like this, sir?" she declared. "You pretend to be won over, which keeps Sir George from playing more tricks such like that one with the necklace."

"But we have just said, Nell . . ." Kate began.

"Let me finish, miss," the abigail replied jumping from one foot to the next in her excitement. "That part would keep her feelings from being

98

hurt, too. Even though she is fond of Mr. Ronhugh, my mistress has her pride, and it would hurt her if she was snubbed."

"You can be certain that no matter what happens I will never snub her," the marquess assured her.

"You've been that good, sir, I can believe you," Nell replied. "All well and good, then. You pay her your attention, and let it come out any way you see fit that you are a scoundrel. Begging your pardon, sir, some gentlemen *are*."

"More than a few," Dev said smiling. "I think, Miss Robinson, that you have hit upon a fine idea. Nothing will suffer but my reputation, and I care very little for that, such as it is. Sir George will see that I am not such a fine catch as he thought, and let his daughter follow her own heart. At least we can hope for that. What think you, Miss Harrison? You have been very quiet."

"That is because I think you are too generous, Lord Gilcrest," Kate said.

"My reputation has suffered before," he told her. "Besides it is in an excellent cause. But you must help me. And you, as well, Miss Robinson. I do not want anyone else involved. Are we agreed?"

"Agreed, sir!" Nell had exclaimed, forgetting herself completely and slapping the marquess on the shoulder.

"For Belinda's sake ... Yes, I agree," Kate said. "Although I do not know what help I can be to you."

And, assuring her that he would think of a plan, Dev had taken his leave.

Belinda's voice roused her to the present.

"But what can Lady Prudence be saying to Papa," the girl demanded, turning from the glass to look at Kate through a tangle of golden curls. "Oh, dear, I hope she has come up with something which will somehow keep him from pressing me on poor Lord Gilcrest."

"If she does not, then someone will," Kate murmured, but in so low a voice that Belinda could not hear.

Nine

"I cannot think what you could have said to Sir George, Mama, to have made him so extremely affable to me when you and he came out of the library," Fitz said as, under Harry's guidance, their carriage rolled down the promenade of packed dirt which bisected the Park. Lady Prudence came here every day with at least one of her sons in tow, it being an excellent thing, she always said, to see and be seen, no matter how much it cut into one's day. As a consequence of this philosophy, they had come here directly from the scene of what her ladyship modestly called her 'triumph' at Sir George Tigford's residence.

The baroness leaned out of the open phaeton to throw a kiss at her dear friend Lady Worthsome who was just rolling past in an ancient but distinguished barouche, before turning to look at her son whose face was set in its usual tragic mask.

"My dear Fitz!" she exclaimed. "Do take that expression off your face. I have been telling you since you were a child that the day will come when you cannot assume a different expression because the facial muscles will be set. Besides, if Sir George was pleasant to you, I think you should be pleased. But doubtless you will find some reason not to be."

"He only meant to throw me off my guard," Fitz muttered.

"Throw you off your guard, you great silly!" his mother said, giving him such a nudge with her elbow that he was nearly propelled from the carriage. "Now why would he want to do that?"

Fitz reached up to set his tricorne hat more securely on his head and ground his teeth together three times before he dared to speak. One day his mother would go too far, although just how far that would have to be he did not know.

"I only know he is a devious gentleman," he replied when his self-possession was quite restored. "Besides, nothing you could have said would have made him like me better, unless you had been in a position to tell him that I had inherited a title and a fortune simultaneously."

"Well, dear," his mother said more mildly. "You cannot blame him for being ambitious for his only daughter. All mamas are the same, and Sir George is behaving as much like a mother hen as any one of them. But of course, given time, he

102

will learn that it is not as easy as it looks to arrange an excellent marriage. There is always some obstacle in the way. Some misconception. As in the case of Lord Gilcrest. Raise your hat to Lady Cantoo, Fitz! And do try not to scowl when you do it."

There was a sudden flutter as several carriages in a row passed their phaeton, all containing various 'dearest' friends, or so Lady Prudence proclaimed, as she threw kisses with abandon and nodded her head until the feathers in her turban drooped wearily.

"Now perhaps you will explain," Fitz said when relative quiet resumed. "What misconception stands in the way of Belinda's marriage to Lord Gilcrest?"

"My dear, you speak about that marriage as though it were a settled fact!" Lady Prudence cried. "And they only met last night! Why must you always be so premature when it comes to trouble?"

Fitz, who believed that by seeking trouble out he could perhaps take it by surprise, did not attempt to explain, since, although his mother delighted in rebuking all her sons, she did not care for self-justification and had when they were children punished them so severely that all four had quite lost the taste for it.

"What was it that you told Sir George, Mama?" Fitz persisted, watching the way the spring sunshine dappled the leaves of the great trees with no show of pleasure on his long face.

Lady Prudence smiled smugly. "The fact is, my dear," she said, "that I simply happened to repeat a few bits of information which I got from Nanny Benbow."

Fitz, who was completely familiar with his mother's old nurse and her penchant for malicious gossip, made the shape of an *O* with his lips.

"It was only a few bits and pieces about Lord Gilcrest," his mother went on. "A few bits and pieces that I did not think he could—as a father, you understand—overlook."

"I suppose you wouldn't care to tell me ..." Fitz began, with such an air of hopelessness that it nearly seemed needless for his mother to reply. Indeed, she only shook her head, whereupon Fitz shook his and Harry, high on the driver's seat, strained his ears, thinking he had missed something of the conversation.

"You know, dear boy, that I am not a gossip," Lady Prudence said primly. "True, I am prepared to be unscrupulous as far as my dear boys are concerned. Yes, indeed, I would see heads roll in every direction to see you all accommodated in the manner you deserve. But to have relayed my little scraps to Sir George was to make all the use of them I care to."

"How did he take the news, pray?" Fitz asked her, wrinkling his forehead in a great scowl.

"Well," Lady Prudence said with relish, "when I made my prelude, he interrupted to say that he knew 'Dev' as he called him, was a scoundrel, and that I could tell him nothing about the lad which would either surprise or shock him."

"Just as I thought," Fitz said in a voice of deep despair. "They will be married, after all."

"Wait! Wait!" his mother cried in irritation. "Why you will always insist on the tragic ending I do not know. Which is not to say that I met with complete success. But then I have never been one to brush aside a compromise."

"You failed, then," Fitz muttered. "Why do you not come straight out and say it, Mama? You always try to put a pretty gloss on everything, but it will not do. The world is a dreadful place. No doubt about it, and it is best to proceed on that assumption. If you do, everything else falls in place."

"I declare I will not tell you, then!" Lady Prudence said in a state of high dudgeon. "If it pleases you to think the worst, then think it! Take us home, Harry, if you please."

Although she did not raise her voice or separate the command from the rest of the conversation, Harry obliged at once, turning the horse's head with energy if no particular skill. A student of human nature, Harry felt that he had found a treasure-trove of idiosyncracies in Lady Prudence's household.

A few minutes passed with the thickest of silences between mother and son. But then, because he wanted so much to know and she to tell, conversation started up again as though it never had been stopped.

"He may have said he could not be shocked or surprised," Lady Prudence remarked, "but I think he was both. Indeed, I am certain of it. Of course, he would pretend otherwise, hemming and hawing and going on with some great nonsense about making a few mistakes when he was young and all the rest. Oh, how he likes to deceive himself! It is, I think, a characteristic of gentlemen of a certain age. I have often noticed it in your father."

"Then your telling Sir George did no good," Fitz said flatly.

"I will admit that took me back a bit," his mother mused, "for had I a daughter and was told what he had been I would have had second thoughts about Lord Gilcrest's eligibility, I assure you. But when I saw how stubborn Sir George meant to be, I took a different tack. You have never known me to be slow-witted, I think, have you, Fitz?"

Difficult as it was for him to make a positive response, her son was forced to admit that that was true.

"I said that of course I knew it would not shock him. That nothing would. I added that he was so absurdly partial to Lord Gilcrest that I thought he would be just as fond if he were to discover that the young man was a murderer."

"And what did he reply to that?"

"La, he was determined to be annoying. He did it deliberately. Laughing and carrying on. He said that if 'Dev' killed someone they were certain to have deserved it, and that he would not hold it a crime. Oh, the man annoys me! He is quite irresponsible. And when Maria was alive she

106

would cater to him so. We knew one another as girls, you see. And she was quite shameless in her pursuit of him. Nothing would do but that she should have him. And once she did, she spent the rest of her life humoring him. That is why he behaves as he does. No one has ever called him a fool. Until today that is."

Fitz could express horror with great sensitivity, engaging not only the eyes and mouth but, by some curious device, making his cheeks hollow in as well. He did so now.

"Mama," he exclaimed, "surely not!"

"But of course I did," Lady Prudence said tartly. "He needs to be told."

"Well then," Fitz said in a disgruntled fashion, "I swear I cannot see what it is you have to be pleased about. He refuses to take whatever scandal you delivered seriously, and then proceeds to lure you on to calling him a fool. And you speak of compromise."

"Harry!" Lady Prudence exclaimed as they rounded a corner nearly on two wheels. "Whatever has gotten into the fellow, I wonder. Give him a poke, Fitz, do. Ah, that is better except that I believe my turban is quite awry. What was I saying?"

"I was saying that I saw very little signs of compromise in what you have told me, Mama," her son said patiently.

"Ah, yes. I told him that it was unfortunate that other people did not take scandal as lightly as he did himself. I said that it would be a pity if, having succeeded in having Belinda woo and win Lord Gilcrest, he was to find that his fine, young marquess could no longer be received in polite society. At first he pretended not to understand me. La! Can you credit that?"

Fitz assured her that he could credit it very well indeed, given the fact that he did not understand it, either. At which Lady Prudence lost her temper completely, called him a lout and boxed his ears, a sight which attracted the attention of a number of passers-by and left Harry, who had witnessed something of what was going on in the phaeton by glances over his shoulder, grinning from ear to ear.

"I told Sir George," Lady Prudence said, hissing the words, "that I would be forced to drop my little bits and pieces of information about Lord Gilcrest here and there and everywhere unless he would be more reasonable. And by that I meant that he should not outlaw you from his household, dear boy. Yes, I was adamant, I assure you. And as a consequence, you are to have a fair chance with your darling Belinda."

Fitz retrieved his tricorne hat from the floor of the carriage where it had fallen when his mother had attacked him. Now, he noted, she was smiling beatifically.

"Dear Fitz," she said. "You will make a good marriage in the end. Oh, I am certain of it. And I will help you in any way I can, just as I have helped your brothers. Now, have I not done a fine thing today? I know there is gratitude lurking under the scowl. Come! Give your mama a kiss and we will be happy together."

Muttering something to the effect that he thought that prediction went too far, Fitz did as he was told, and mother and son settled back in their seats to share the excitement of traveling down Piccadilly with Harry at the reins.

Ten

"It is always a mistake, I think," Sir George declared, "to rest after a victory."

Kate and Belinda who sat beside the round table in the sitting room, busy with their embroidery in the soft candlelight, raised their heads warily and exchanged glances of trepidation. Perhaps because it was Sunday, Sir George had not said a word as yet about what he now called his Grand Design. As they were on their way home from church, Belinda had whispered that she was beginning to think that whatever Lady Prudence had said to her father had put him off. But Kate had guessed that her cousin was being too optimistic, and now she saw that she had been only too right.

"Last Friday evening Lord Gilcrest was intrigued," Sir George continued in the deep voice

111

which he always assumed when he was pontificating. "But I fear we may have had a false sense of victory, my dear Belinda, since the gentleman has not subsequently called."

Kate turned her face away at that, afraid her uncle might see her flush. She had not been quite certain until now that the tip which she had sent via Nell to Tom, the footman, had been sufficient to guarantee his silence about Dev's visit. But now it was quite clear that Sir George knew nothing about it. What would he think, she wondered, if he knew that she had entertained Lord Gilcrest for nearly an hour with his daughter's abigail as her only chaperone? What would he say if he knew that she had met Dev four years ago and that, like the foolish girl she had been then, she had fancied herself in love?

"Dear Papa," she heard Belinda say, "isn't it possible that Lord Gilcrest prefers to see a—a wide variety of ladies? I mean that certainly he was most attentive to me on Friday, but that was only to make up for the cruel sport his friends had made of me. I think that ordinarily he gads about as they do, and you must have noticed that none of them danced with the same partner the entire evening."

In her innocence she had said the worst thing possible, Kate thought. Such a comment would only serve to stir her father up. Hoping to distract him, Kate ventured to ask about Lady Prudence.

"She seemed to be so full of something, Uncle," she concluded. "But then, I expect that it is secret."

She, too, had better have remained silent, Kate saw at once, for Sir George reared up in his chair and nearly knocked the decanter of port which stood on the table beside him to the floor.

"Blasted woman!" he exclaimed. "Always with her finger in some pie or other! But she has not been as clever as she thought. Although, now that I think on it, she did get what she wanted."

"Please, Papa," Belinda said. "I cannot think what you are talking of."

"Blackmail is the name for it!" her father roared. "The old muckworm thinks she can make things a bit awkward for me. No matter how. That does not signify. But I only laughed at her, you know. Nothing shocks me! Nothing! But then she went a step further. Turned the screw, don't you know? I thought it politic to give in, then. But only on a small point."

"May I ask what the small point was, Papa?" Belinda asked. "May we know that, at least?"

"Why, you cannot complain of my lack of frankness," Sir George declared. "Never was a man more open than I am, I think. The fact is that in return for her—er, discretion, I agreed that Fitz could be about the place on occasion. No need for him to turn down balls at which you will be at, my dear. That sort of thing."

"Oh, Papa!" Belinda cried, dropping her embroidery hoop and running to hug her father so enthusiastically that she nearly dislodged his great, black wig.

"What's this, eh? What's this?" he sputtered, pulling himself to rights. "You quite mistake me,

Child, if you think I will allow you to continue your flirtation with that wretched young man. Why, even if he had money and a title coming to him, I should think twice, for I have never seen a fellow more down at the mouth than he, although the fact that Lady Prudence is his mother may be some part of the explanation. I would be depressed myself. Indeed I would."

And with that Sir George paused to take his snuff-box from his pocket and proceed with the ritual which the two girls knew better than to interrupt. Only when he had sneezed resoundingly five times in succession did Belinda dare to speak again. She had returned to her chair and taken up her embroidery and now she sat staring at her father with a most mournful expression.

"So you mean," she said, "that I am not to dance with Fitz or hold a conversation."

"I shall not be pleased if I see you doing so," Sir George replied. "In the first place, it will make Lord Gilcrest think that you are not particular when you select your friends."

"I do not think the marquess is such a snob as that, Papa," Belinda protested.

"And if we speak of the quality of one's friends," Kate interjected, "I think his own would not endure a close perusal."

"I will not be contradicted!" Sir George declared, rising to his feet and walking to the fire where he stood with the darting light glistening against the big buckles of his shoes, an awe-inspiring figure in brown satin pantaloons with his hands gripped under the long tails of his elegant frock coat.

"I would never think of contradicting you, Papa," Belinda said in a very small voice indeed. "I only wish you could appreciate Fitz's virtues."

"I was not aware that he possessed any of significance, miss," Sir George replied. "Now, we will say no more of Fitz this evening, do you hear? And I want you to attend to what I have to say."

But first, it seemed, he must pour himself a glass of port, giving time for Kate to reflect on what he had to say about Lady Prudence's visit. Blackmail had been mentioned. And he had spoken of guaranteeing her discretion by allowing Fitz to be about Belinda sometimes.

There were, Kate thought, too few pieces of the puzzle to put them together properly. But she could make some sort of guess. Someone's reputation was clearly at stake. It could not be Belinda's, since if one were to discount the breaking of her necklace she had never done anything out of the way.

Was it possible, Kate wondered, that Lady Prudence had discovered something about Sir George's past which she had threatened to reveal. Certainly he prided himself on having been something of a scamp when he was young, but, as far as Kate knew, he had led a proper life ever since he had married. In fact she thought that it was the restlessness produced by the restraints of being so very proper which had induced him to play this absurd game, using his daughter as a pawn. No, it did not seem likely that Lady Prudence could be blackmailing him directly.

Who else was left? No one that Kate could think of except ... That must be it, of course! Lady Prudence knew something about Dev and had promised to be discreet if she could be assured that Fitz would no longer be banished completely. Oh, if that could only be the case, what good fortune it would be, since nothing could fit in better with Dev's plan. Whatever Lady Prudence had managed to collect in the way of scandal, it had clearly not been enough to put Sir George off. And that meant ... why, it meant that it would be advantageous to know precisely what she had reported, in order to determine the limit of bad behavior on Dev's part which Sir George was willing to put up with.

But how to find out what Lady Prudence had told him? If it went against Dev, there was no use hoping that her uncle might be beguiled into reporting anything against his favorite. Lady Prudence had presumably promised to hold her tongue, and Fitz had certainly never demonstrated that he could manipulate his mother in any way. But perhaps he could find out where she had gotten her information.

All of this was based on an uncertain premise, and Kate did not intend to forget it. But she had promised to help Dev convince Sir George that he was not a suitable husband for Belinda, and she must as a consequence take even the most uncertain path. Yes, she would talk to Fitz. Now that he had been readmitted into Belinda's presence, he was certain to accompany his mother on her daily visit to the Tigford residence tomorrow. How fortunate it was that Sir George was not so particular about who she talked to as he was Belinda, Kate thought. Indeed, she should be more grateful than she was that his Grand Design occupied him to such an extent that he scarcely noticed what she was about.

"Now then," Sir George said, raising his glass of port as though he meant to toast himself, "I have an excellent idea as to how we should proceed."

"Proceed in what, Papa?" Belinda said innocently, and glancing at her cousin, Kate thought that she was learning something of delaying tactics, even if outright disobedience seemed destined to elude her.

"In my Grand Design to help you win my friend Dev for a husband," Sir George replied impatiently. "What else should I be speaking of?"

Kate wanted to reply that nearly anything he could think of would be more appropriate, but she held her tongue.

"Do you know, Papa," Belinda said, "now that I have met Lord Gilcrest, I think that I am prepared to say that, although he is certainly handsome and as charming as any gentleman I have ever met . . ."

"As well as being titled and possessing a fortune of some considerable magnitude," her father reminded her.

"Yes, yes. I have not forgotten the title and the fortune, Papa. Indeed, even if I wanted to, you

117

would not let me do it. But what I meant to say was that I believed I have seen enough of Lord Gilcrest to know that he is not for me."

Lord George, who was sipping his port as she spoke, began to sputter. "You put too high a value on your own character, gel!" he exclaimed.

"Oh, I do not mean that I think myself better than he," Belinda protested. "Indeed, it is clear that he exceeds me in intelligence and wit and sophistication and . . . and any number of things. As many as you could think to name. And that is just the point. Even if I did pretend to be someone, I am not long enough to interest him— although, I do not think that possible—he would soon learn how different I am from him and from his friends. Indeed, he must know it already for, although you sent me off on Friday provided with a daring gown and a necklace to break, you made no provision, dear Papa, for my conversation with him after we had met. I declare I did not know what he was speaking of more often than not, and I think I missed some of his jokes as well, for he has a sense of irony like Kate, and you know how often I miss the point of what she is saying completely."

She paused breathless as Sir George, whose face looked like a Christmas pudding on the boil, first growing fat and puffy and then seeming to fall in on itself, made a growling sound deep in his throat.

"No more, chit!" he cried when his convulsion was over. "I want to hear no more of that sort of talk. If Lord Gilcrest had found anything about

118

you to dislike at the ball on Friday, he would have left you straight away. Remember, he was under no obligation . . ."

"No doubt he thought he was under a moral obligation, Papa," Belinda cried desperately. "I tell you that I am certain that he stayed with me to make up for the way his friends behaved. He felt sorry for me, Papa. Sorry!"

"Enough!" Sir George roared in such a voice that both girls started up from their chairs. "Sit down!" was his next command which they obeyed promptly. "Sit down and listen to me!"

"Now," Sir George went on when it was so quiet in the room that his heavy breathing sounded like a bellows. "I will have no more impertinence from either of you."

Kate wanted to remind him that she had not said a word, but decided that this was not the time to insist on absolute accuracy. Neither was it the time, she sensed, to leave the room, even though that idea was a tempting one. Clearly, Belinda needed someone sympathetic close to her, and besides her uncle was in such a mood that it seemed prudent to remain quite motionless. Furthermore, she had told Dev that she would keep him informed as to further plans so that he would be prepared to respond appropriately. Remembering that made her heart stop for a moment, as she imagined what would happen could her uncle read her mind. She did not like to think what he would say or do if he knew that she was playing the role of spy now.

Never having thought of it in precisely those

terms before, Kate was suddenly plunged into a slough of guilt. Is this the way she repaid someone who had given her her coming-out? It was beside the point that she had not wanted to come-out in the first place. He had been generous with his time and money. There was no gainsaying that. And this was the way she was rewarding him?

But the rationale came tiptoeing close on the heels of the argument. She was doing this because of her friendship for Belinda, because she wanted her cousin to be happy, even if her conception of happiness was life with dismal Fitz. A bit encouraged by this thought, Kate sat as straight up in her chair as Belinda was doing and listened to Sir George deliver a philippic at the close of which, an hour later, Belinda's next ploy, to be used at Lady Lingerlong's on Monday night, had been carefully delineated.

"But I cannot behave that way," Belinda whispered to Kate when, having delivered himself, her father left the room. "Did you hear what he had to say about how I should play the flirt in order to make Lord Gilcrest jealous? If it had not been so dreadful, I should have laughed to see him show me how to hold my fan just below my eyes and flutter my lashes up and down. And was it not absurd when he told me how to giggle? Oh, it is wrong of me, I know, Kate, but I feel so strange. One part of me is horrified, and the other wants to laugh and laugh until I cry."

"I liked it best when your father showed you how to lure young gentlemen on," Kate said mischievously. "Oh dear, I had to bite my lip when he went mincing across the floor, pretending to be holding up his skirts ever so slightly and giving such a fetching smile over his shoulder. Perhaps it was because of his black wig. Or perhaps it was because he is so tall, but really it was . . ."

She could not finish for laughter's sake, and soon the cousins were clutching one another, convulsed by a hilarity which luckily Sir George, in his room above, did not hear.

Eleven

The next morning, when Lady Prudence arrived with Fitz in tow and ready to accompany the girls to Madame LeClare's in order to fit Belinda to a new gown or two, Kate made a point to sit next to Fitz in the carriage, and while his mother and Belinda were chatting about the advisability of having a pelisse made to match the gown, she told him that she must speak to him alone.

Typically, Fitz's first response was to declare that he did not see how that would be possible since there were four in the party. At that Kate, always much amused by his dark view of life, proposed that since neither he nor she was to be measured by Madame LeClare for a new gown, a private discussion between the two of them was not beyond the realm of possibility.

As it turned out it was an even simpler matter

than Kate had imagined, since it developed that Madame had exercised rather more of her own judgment than Lady Prudence thought desirable in regard to the cut of the bodice. It was useless for her to protest that, since Sir George had been adamant about the décolletage of the last gown she had composed for Mademoiselle, she had assumed that that would be rule for all the others, but since she was a voluble Frenchwoman, protest she did; both in her own language and in English and finally in a combination of both.

While this was going on in the fitting room, Fitz and Kate were left quite undisturbed in an adjacent chamber and she had lost no time in making her point with him.

"But my mother refused to tell me what she said to Sir George," he protested as soon as Kate had asked her question. "She will never tell me anything of importance, you know. I know it was some scandal or other but that won't help you much, will it?"

Kate confessed that it would not, and then went on to make delicate enquiries as to where Lady Prudence might have gathered her information, only to be told by Fitz that, in his opinion, this was not a proper conversation.

"Mama may shove me about a bit," he said, scowling, "but that is only for my own good. What sort of son would I be if I were to talk about her behind her back, I ask you?"

At that Kate proposed that he would be a very sensible son indeed, since she had reason to think that the scandal concerned Lord Gilcrest and that it would be to Fitz's advantage to have her stir the matter about a bit.

"Sir George may not be upset by it," she said. "But perhaps there is more where that came from." At that Fitz almost smiled, although he prevented himself from doing so at the last moment and with considerable effort. She must let him think, he said, and think he did, falling into the brownest study that Kate had ever witnessed.

"I think," Fitz said at last, "that Mama said she had a few bits and pieces from Nanny Benbow."

An explanation then being in order, Fitz told Kate the odd story of his mother's old nurse.

"When my grandfather died," he said dourly, "he left the old lady well set up. In fact, a good part of the money which should have come to Mama went to her, on account of his thinking Mama had married beneath her, which of course she did."

He paused to contemplate this satisfying misfortune for so long that Kate became afraid that Lady Prudence and Madame LeClare would settle their differences before he had time to finish.

"How fascinating," she urged.

Fitz threw her a look which indicated that he would have chosen another adjective.

"And where is—Nanny Benbow now?" Kate asked him. Whereupon Fitz explained that the old lady had satisfied an old ambition by purchasing a house just off Grosvenor Square where, by means of the constant entertainment of a variety of old acquaintances who were still in service in the households of the *haut ton,* she kept herself well abreast of the gossip which was her life's blood.

On closer examination, Kate was able to extract the information that, far from being content with old friends alone, Nanny Benbow who seemed, she thought, an extremely enterprising old woman, often solicited information from further afield, letting it be known in fact that she was not averse, were the information scandalous enough, to paying hard cash for it.

"Oh dear!" Kate exclaimed, genuinely shocked, "Do you think your grandfather realized what use she would make of the money he left her?"

"Dash it, she told him often enough," Fitz replied. "Or so Mama claims. He had a peculiar sense of humor, you see. And he liked his bit of gossip even though he lived in the country. Mama declares that Nanny Benbow made an addict of him, in a manner of speaking. According to her, Nanny Benbow let my grandfather know that she would never confide another bit of scandal to him unless he made provisions in his will accordingly. Mama says that it is all so outrageous that she cannot think of it without developing a megrim."

"And yet she sees her old nurse sometimes," Kate said quickly. "Indeed, you said she had her 'bits and pieces' about Lord Gilcrest from her."

"Mama is always practical," Fitz replied with a pensive scowl. "My father says she'd bargain with the devil if she thought it would be to her advantage."

Kate smiled pleasantly at this expression of parental respect, and set herself to thinking of ways by which she could, either directly or indirectly, put herself in touch with the extraordinary old lady who had established such a profitable marketplace for scandal. It did not take her long to think of possibilities, and Lady Prudence's battle with Madame was still in full swing long after she had made her plan.

Nell, however, when Kate approached her later, was appalled by the idea, although she did admit that Nanny Benbow's reputation had reached her ears.

"I hear she either takes her information in guineas or exchange," she said, rolling her eyes. "Ain't it dreadful, miss, what some folk will stoop to?"

"But think what a good cause it would be in, in our case, Nell," Kate replied. "You heard what Lord Gilcrest said. He only wants to help my cousin out of her difficulties. And you know how fond she is of Mr. Ronhugh."

"La, I can't fancy what she sees in him, miss," Nell declared, "although it's not my place to say it, I'm sure. Surly sort of fellow, ain't he?"

Having assured the abigail that it was not for them to question the object of Belinda's affection, Kate dug about in a little box that she kept at the back of her dressing table drawer and brought out two shining guineas.

"That should be enough to purchase the information that we want," she said briskly. "Simply say that you wish to know the very worst she knows about Lord Gilcrest. The *very* worst, you understand. Nothing less will do."

But it required more than briskness to convince Nell that what she was being asked to do was proper, and it was the middle of the afternoon before Kate saw her off, still muttering to herself, in the direction of Nanny Benbow's address, which Kate had taken care to have exactly from Fitz earlier.

There being nothing left to do but wait, Kate occupied her time at first with her own doubts as to the wisdom of what she was doing. It had seemed a simple matter, at the time, to agree to Dev's suggestion that he present himself in such a light as to make it impossible for Sir George to consider him a possible husband for Belinda. Now she reminded herself that Dev had not asked her to take an active part in the affair. What would he think when he discovered that she had allowed herself to be carried away by her enthusiasm to the extent that she had actually sent one of Sir George's servants to gather scandal about him? Indeed, it occurred to Kate that he might not be at all pleased. But surely when she told him that Lady Prudence had already made an attempt to disenchant Sir George, Dev would see the wisdom of what she had done. Certainly he should know precisely how bad a reputation he must assume in order to influence her uncle.

Forced to content herself with these reassurances, Kate sought escape from her own thoughts by seeking company, only to find that Sir George had closeted Belinda in the library and was engaged in putting her to practicing the wiles she was to display that evening.

"Ah, Kate, my dear!" he cried when she appeared at the door. "The very person we want! Belinda has been telling me that I am too fond of exaggerated behavior. The poor child is too conservative by far, and can think of nothing except her modesty. Let modesty go hang, I tell her, but you know what she is."

Behind her uncle's back, Kate gave her cousin a glance of encouragement before she took the wing chair Sir George pulled forward and became the audience.

"Now, my dear," Sir George told his daughter, "we will run through the minuet again. I will hum the tune so that we may keep to the beat. Now, I bow and you curtsy. Tra la la. Tra la la. No, indeed, Belinda! That will not do at all. I have told you time and time again that you must languish with your eyes as you sink to the floor, and raise your fan to hide your mouth. There must be more of the voluptuous about it."

"Oh, Papa!" Belinda cried, raising her fan to cover her entire face. "How I do wish you would not speak so."

"You must be ravishing, my dear! Ravishing!" Sir George exclaimed. "Dev is a hot-blooded young man, you know, not one of your ordinary fops. No doubt a Spanish dance would suit him better, but since we are in London we must make what we can of what we have. And what we have is the minuet. Give me your fan. Observe me curtsy. Mark how I lower my eyes, thus. Do you not see the sensuous quality?"

Kate tried, but she could not help herself. She laughed until there was a great pain in her side. She kept on laughing until tears were streaming down her cheeks. She laughed and laughed until she did not think she could draw another breath. And when, at last, she was in control enough to look about her, she saw that Belinda was laughing, too, having thrown herself into a chair and stuffed a handkerchief into her mouth. Sir George surveyed the scene with outraged eyes, still holding his daughter's fan.

It was the first time he had been angry with Kate, and she was sorry for it. Indeed, she apologized as soon as she could speak. But Sir George was not mollified.

"Your sense of humor has led you astray in this particular instance," he said, red-faced with the attempt to restrain himself from losing all control. "You make a mockery of things. It will not do, miss. From now on I will rehearse my daughter in private. Please to leave us alone directly."

As she left the room, Kate looked back to see a sobered Belinda sitting very upright in her chair, her golden head bowed, ready to receive her own rebuke. And, although Kate knew that her behavior had been unpardonable, she vowed to deliver her cousin from her father's mad scheme.

As a consequence, it was with relief that she

found a clearly rattled Nell waiting for her in the hall outside her room.

"Oh, miss," the abigail declared when they were alone together, "such a time I had."

"She wanted more than the two guineas?" Kate demanded in disbelief.

"No, miss," Nell replied, taking off her bonnet, "but she is such a strange old woman. She wanted to know all about me, and I was afraid that if she knew I was a servant for Sir George . . ."

"Quite right," Kate said impatiently. "Did you tell her?"

"Not I, miss," Nell declared. "But I have never had to lie so straight ahead as I have this past hour. I made up a name and said my master was straight from the Continent, and then she said that she must know why I wanted the information. I declare, it makes my head spin just to think of it."

"What reason did you give her?" Kate said sharply.

"I said I was not certain, but I thought that Lord Gilcrest had managed to dishonor my master's sister. Oh, miss, it was the first thing that came to mind! Was not that awful of me?"

"I think it may have been very clever," Kate said with a smile. "I expect she wanted details."

"Indeed she did!" Nell exclaimed. "And I said that I was not certain of them, but if she wanted I would make a collection of facts and bring them to her on another occasion. La, she was that excited! She had me spell my master's name three times and . . ."

"But did she tell you what you wanted to know?" Kate demanded. "That is the important thing."

Nell closed her eyes and put her thoughts in order. "There were four things, miss," she said with a blink. "First, Lord Gilcrest is overfond of deep basset, and once lost a thousand pounds at a sitting."

"Yes," Kate said. "What else? What else?"

"And once he disappointed a lady who swore that he had offered for her."

"What else?" Kate demanded.

"He fought a duel in Virginia and scarred the other gentleman on the cheek."

"And is there more?"

"Once, in his cups, he climbed to the top of the wall at St. James's Palace and walked about on the top singing until the guards had him down. If it had not been for his father, he might have gone to the gaols for that, miss."

"Is there more?" Kate demanded, finding herself quite breathless. And why? Because she was afraid that Nell would tell her something quite unpardonable, some outright crime, some viciousness. But why should she care so much?

"That's the lot, miss," Nell replied, puffing out her cheeks. "Poof! I wasn't half on my nerves! The old lady puts me in a jitter, and no mistake!"

"But there must be more!" Kate cried, hiding her relief. "Did you tell her you wanted to know the very worst?"

Nell nodded. " 'Pon my soul, I did, miss. But that was all she knew, and I fancy she is honest

132

enough in her way. But there! You must be disappointed."

"Not I!" Kate cried, seizing the girl in a moment of exhilaration and spinning her about the floor. "I may be many things, but I am not disappointed!"

Twelve

It was strange, Kate thought, that although she
had only been a few weeks in London it began to
seem that one ballroom was very like another.
Even her hostesses seemed to be assuming a
mysterious similarity, and certainly there was no
question that the other guests were one and the
same. One could be certain that old Lord Kneeup
would be trying to pinch pretty girls in a corner,
and that the Duchess of Woodstill would be telling anyone who could bear to listen the latest
details of the condition of her health, which seemed
to be always so precarious that it could only be
wondered how it was that Her Grace managed
never to miss a public function. But this reflection did not occupy Kate's mind for long since her
main purpose for standing near the stairs in order
to watch each new arrival was to intercept Dev

as soon as he arrived, and before her uncle was able to set Belinda on her reluctant pursuit of him.

As she watched the guests arrive, the gentlemen bending over their hostess's hand and the ladies, more often than not, embracing her and gushing endearments, Kate felt like a plain sparrow among a group of peacocks. It was not that her dress was drab, for Lady Prudence, although not spending as much care and time with Sir George's niece as she did his daughter, had seen to it that Kate had a small but stylish wardrobe. Tonight, for instance, she had chosen a gown of blue and silver stripes with an underskirt of forthy lace which matched that at her bodice. Although Sir George had protested, she had drawn the line completely at the powdering of her hair this evening, and the red blaze of her curls contrasted violently with the elegant white pompadours which surrounded her. It was, she knew, a silly protest, but it made her feel as though she had clung to some of her own identity. No matter how finely gowned she was, she knew she could never be a real part of these preening, posturing, posing people who surrounded her.

But what troubled her most at the moment was Dev. If he were to come into the ballroom with his swaggering companions with him, all attention would be drawn to the door, and there would be no possibility of her speaking to him in private. Probably it was typical of his thoughtlessness that he had neglected to deal with this small detail when they had made their plan.

"If you will only let me know what your uncle plans as a ploy on the particular evenings when we chance to attend the same entertainment, I will be prepared to deal with it," he had said.

Now, Kate wondered if he had meant that he should be informed by letter. That would, of course, be the most private way, but somehow it seemed too much like an intrigue to think of doing so. And yet, she reflected, they *had* intrigued, *must* intrigue if they hoped to protect Belinda.

Two dandies with quizzing glasses raised to their eyes paused as they passed her, and Kate heard one exclaim that she was a 'demned beauty,' while the other replied that he had heard that she delighted in making 'lobcocks' of gentlemen like themselves who affected the latest styles. Although she pretended not to hear, Kate was pleased that she had, it seemed, won herself a particular reputation for being unsympathetic with the foppish set.

And then, quite suddenly, Dev's friends streamed into the room with so much good looks and boldness about them that you could hear the cooes rise from the ladies as though a dovecote had been invaded. But where was Dev? Kate asked herself. He was not leading them, as he had before, nor was he one of their number. Just as it had before the attention of the entire room focused on them, and at that moment Kate felt someone touch her arm.

She turned and gave a little cry, for it was Dev. Dressed in gray satin tonight, he was the picture of elegance, although like herself his hair was quite unpowdered. He beckoned her to a little alcove, half hidden by drapes, and Kate followed quickly.

"I have been waiting for the proper moment, Miss Harrison," he said as they stood close together in the shadows, quite sheltered from the ballroom. "I knew my friends would provide their customary distraction. I hope you have not forgotten what we agreed to."

Kate's heart had risen in her mouth when she had turned and seen him so unexpectedly, but now she had had time to compose herself. Certainly she felt quite secure here, for she was certain that her uncle's attention would have been caught by the crowd of young men, and that even now he was probably seeking out Dev among them.

"No," she said. "I did not forget. Indeed, I have accomplished another bit of business which will assist you. But first, about tonight. My uncle has been drilling my cousin in a minuet."

"But surely she knows the steps of such an ordinary dance," Dev replied, raising his dark eyebrows. "In fact, I know she does, for I danced one with her the other evening."

Kate had not thought she would find it so difficult to explain. At the time she had seen her uncle prancing and languishing about she had not been able to keep from laughing, but now all she could remember was the look on her cousin's face much later when the session was over.

"What can I do?" she had cried over and over.

"I shall make a fool of myself if I do the things he tells me to!"

"Then disobey him," Kate had said in a low voice. "Say no. Perhaps it is wrong for me to say it, but I think a father should be obeyed to the point that he follows common sense, and not a step further."

But that advice had seemed to rattle Belinda even more, and Kate had left off trying to persuade her at once. She had been sorely tempted then to confide in her cousin, to tell her at the very least that Lord Gilcrest was sympathetic to her plight, and that he only sought to make matters easier for her until he could find a way to persuade her papa that he was not the gentleman to offer for her. One thing and one thing alone had held her back, and that was the fear that, dutiful as she was and always had been, Belinda would go to her father with the news. Or even if she could be sworn to secrecy, it was all too likely, Kate thought, that her cousin might, quite unintentionally, let out a hint or two.

"She has been drilled to act in a most flirtatious manner when she does the minuet with me, then?" Dev said when Kate had finally, and with all the delicacy she possessed, made herself clear. "I think from the few details you have given me that there is every likelihood that she would make herself absurd. Indeed, I am coming to wonder if Sir George sees the world as it really is, or as he would like it to be. No doubt all of us gentlemen would be pleased to see ladies draping themselves

139

about at every turn and batting their eyes like bats' wings, but that is not the way of it."

"He is recalling the way his wife flirted with him," Kate replied. "And, in his imagination he has blown up her mannerisms out of all proportion. Then, too, there may be something in what you have to say, as well, for he is a gentleman who sees what he prefers to see. Perhaps you should know that I urged her to defy him, but she cannot bring herself to it."

"Well, well," Dev murmured. "I will think of a way to keep her off the dance floor for the evening. And it should be an easy enough matter, by sitting on the sidelines and making certain comments on the ladies who dance by, to convince Sir George that I like the modest decorum best. What think you of that, Miss Harrison?"

"Why, if you can accomplish it 'twill be a fine thing, sir," Kate replied. "It is an excellent thought to let my uncle know you do not care for boldness on the dance floor, but first you must keep my cousin off it until my uncle is persuaded. She has been advised to act in the manner I described, you see, whether she dances with you or some other. The purpose is for you to see . . ."

The words were difficult to find, but when she groped for them, he put her at her ease by interrupting to assure her that he understood.

"I will ask your cousin to sit out the first minuet," Dev told her. "It seems that I have wrenched my leg and require cosseting. And while she and Sir George keep me company, I will deliver myself of my notions about the dignity which the minuet requires and our problems should be solved for the evening."

"It is good of you to take these pains to protect her," Kate told him, speaking very quickly now for the musicians were tuning up and she knew they could not spend much longer in conversation. "I have one other thing to say to you."

It seemed to Kate that he moved closer then, and perhaps he did if only to hear her better, since she spoke in a low voice. At all events, he seemed very near to her there in the shadows, so close that his dark eyes were hooded when he looked at her.

"You may not approve of what I have done, sir," Kate said in as businesslike a tone as she could manage. "Indeed it would not have occurred to me to have made so bold had it not been for a curious coincidence to the effect that, at the very time you were considering ways of demonstrating to my uncle that you were not a suitable object of my cousin's affections, Lady Prudence had the same idea."

"Lady Prudence?" he said frowning. "I am afraid, Miss Harrison, that I know no one by that name unless—but, yes, of course! You must mean the Baroness Ronhugh. The lady with the eligible sons, whose names all begin with *F*. The *haut ton* is so exclusive one cannot help but know everyone, you see."

He spoke with such wryness that Kate could not help but smile. However different their way of life was, Dev at least shared her feelings about the *beau monde*.

141

"And," he continued, "if I recall correctly, Miss Robinson—I hope the lady is quite well—happened to mention when I was with you the other day that your cousin is attached to one of the Ronhugh brothers. Given Miss Tigford's rumored fortune, I expect the mother has been encouraging the connection."

He spoke with so much bitterness that Kate was startled, and suddenly she remembered that day in the autumn-crusted meadow when they had first met. Had he not said then that he would like to leave all this? And yet here he was trapped in it once more. But that was something that she dared not comment on, she told herself. The only reason there was any intimacy between them was because of Belinda, and she would be a fool to forget it.

"Lady Prudence would certainly be pleased to see an alliance made between her youngest son and my cousin," Kate replied. "I would not speak of this if it were not necessary in order to explain certain things to you."

"I believe you in that," Dev said with a curious expression in his dark eyes. "You are the sort to keep your own counsel for the most part, I think."

Kate overlooked the comment, and continued. "My cousin's fortune may have encouraged Lady Prudence to support the match," she said, "but my cousin is truly fond of Fitz and he of her, although given his nature, he cannot believe that anything will come of it. But that is beside the point."

"Nothing is beside the point when you speak of

it," Dev said in a low voice and Kate was certain that he stood much closer to her now. She could not take a step back without endangering exposure to the public gaze, and she thought angrily that no doubt it amused him to tease her in this fashion, knowing her to be a simple country girl.

"I am afraid that you are crowding me, sir," she said tartly. "I think it is important for you to know what I intend to say, but I will not continue unless you will put a greater distance between us."

Dev laughed, but there was an expression of admiration on his handsome face, and he did as she requested.

"I like the way you speak directly to the point," he said.

"It is a quaint country custom," Kate said dryly. "But now, if you do not mind, I will proceed. Lady Prudence is a friend of my uncle as well, and offered generously to undertake certain duties connected with my cousin and my coming out. Therefore it was only to be expected that she should hear my uncle's plan concerning you, sir, and quite natural that she should try to put a stop to it in her own particular way."

"Ah yes," Dev said in a low voice. "Quite natural. I hesitate to think how she went about it."

Perhaps it was the hint of something like desolation in his voice which made Kate tell him precisely what Lady Prudence had done, and where she had found the information that she wanted. Certainly, she had not intended to do so. But then, she had meant to be suitably vague about all of this. The impulse to be totally open with Dev was very strong and, she thought, dangerous, in some way that she did not completely understand.

"Just when you think that everything about this society is utterly familiar, you learn something new," he said with a hard note to his voice. "Usually, I must confess, that new something is unpleasant. I daresay I should simply call this absurd and be done with it. A retired nanny who trades in scandal. Yes, the more I think of it the more possible it becomes that, given time, I may laugh."

There were, Kate saw, darker waters to him than she had guessed, and she hurried on, afraid that if she were to delay she might not gather up the courage to continue. Strange that she had not expected him to be shocked by what Nanny Benbow was doing. Surely he was sophisticated enough to be cynical about everything. Indeed, Kate was certain that if she remained in London for the entire Season, nothing would amaze her.

"Sir George would not say what she had told him," she went on quickly, "except that it concerned your reputation, sir. Whatever it was, he professed not to be shocked by it. You will be glad to know that you are still his scoundrel and his scamp."

"Delightful," Dev said with a wry smile. He had stepped away from her at her command, Kate noted, but not far enough to say they had reached more than a simple compromise as to positioning.

"But you see," Kate went on, "it made me think. I know you hope to make your reputation appear bad enough to discourage my uncle in his ambitions. And it occurred to me that, if I were to find out what Lady Prudence reported to him, I would better know what sort of enormities you would presumably have had to have committed to put you beyond the pale."

"You are very clever, Miss Harrison," he said, his dark eyes on hers. The music could be heard now playing the first cotillion, and Kate knew that she must be faster still. In rapid summary, she told of sending Nell to Nanny Benbow, and now at last he was amused.

"But come!" he said. "You must tell me more of this. How extraordinarily shrewd of you! How did your cousin's abigail explain why she wanted the information about me? She must be someone on whom you can depend. But wait! I think I can guess her other name. Tell me, Miss Harrison, is it not Robinson?"

Kate confessed that it was so, and would have gone on with her story if Dev had not insisted on continuing to be amused. And when she finally recited the four bits of scandal held against him, he was still in a high humor, although precisely why she could not suppose.

"Well, if Sir George will not be put off by duelling, drunkenness, gambling and unfaithfulness, I am at a loss as to what to do unless I commit a murder," he declared. "Tell me, Miss Harrison, is that what I am to do?"

There was something about his tone Kate did not like. Did he think that he could be familiar with her now that she had involved herself as

145

she had? Worse, had he assumed that she, like all the other women of his acquaintance, was so struck by him that she would go out of her way to help him? Kate did not know whether it was his fault she felt this sudden, deep humiliation, or her own. She only knew she could not stay with him for another moment, exchange another word.

And so she left him, slipped around the curtain and melted into the crowd. It was too late to take part in the cotillion, but a young viscount whom she had found attentive on several other occasions, begged to take her arm for a stroll on the terrace and Kate agreed. The last thing she saw before they left the ballroom was Dev approaching Sir George and Belinda, hindered in his progress by a decided limp.

Thirteen

On Tuesday it rained, and when Kate went into the library after breakfast to find a book she found Fitz sitting by one of the long windows, his face a perfect metaphor for the gloom outside. It took more than one question, to be sure, but finally she deduced that Lady Prudence had left him there, much as one might leave a dog in the anteroom, while she was with Belinda upstairs on some business or other, otherwise generalized by Fitz into 'nonsense.' Feeling sorry for him, and if truth be told much in need of distraction herself, Kate took the leather chair across from him and tried to stir up a conversation.

But it took a very long spoon, indeed, to stir up anything with Fitz, until she stumbled on the subject of the ball of the night before. Seeing him sit up straighter in his chair and assume even a

147

more miserable expression than formerly, Kate guessed she had struck on a nerve. And, although the subject of last night was painful to her as well, she pursued it ruthlessly.

"It's clear she means to marry him," Fitz burst out before Kate had gone very far with her talk of what so-and-so was wearing and how someone else had behaved. "No need to contradict me, for I was there to see it with my own eyes."

Assuming that he was referring to Belinda, Kate suggested that although Lord Gilcrest certainly had been attentive, that was not necessarily agreeable to Belinda, and if she had sat all the dances out because of Lord Gilcrest's lameness it was only because her father had given her no alternative.

"Be fair," she persisted. "You could have come to ask her for a dance, but you did not. Why was that, pray?"

Whereupon Fitz had grumbled something about Sir George having his head if he had so much as come in his direction.

"He would have had to let her dance with you," Kate declared. "You know that as well as I do. Remember the arrangement that was made with your mother."

That had alerted his interest to the extent of making him enquire how it was she knew of the arrangement, and that he was not privy to the details of that arrangement himself. To all of which Kate replied that she knew as little as he, but surely he had been told that the former restrictions against him had been removed. The very fact of his having been found sitting in Sir George's library was proof enough of that.

"Surely," she said, "your mother has told you how far you may go."

Fitz, grim-jawed, replied that it was all very well telling him that Lord George would have him in the house, but what good would that do when Belinda had been warned not to be found in his vicinity, and not to engage him in conversation at any time?

"But how do you know that?" Kate demanded.

"Because your cousin wrote to me," Fitz declared. "Her father said nothing about writing, you see. But he will find out soon enough, I'm certain. No doubt you will tell him. And then he will forbid her even that."

Kate considered reading him a lecture on the subject of looking on the bright side, and then decided against it. True, this conversation was distracting her from her own troubles, but it was also depressing and frustrating her so severely that it might well have been better to brood alone. But, having opened one of Fitz's numerous Pandora's boxes of despair, she felt obliged to offer some advice.

"If you thought there was a possibility that I might inform against you, surely it was foolhardy to tell me what you did," she said. "I think that the trouble you already have is not enough to keep you from fabricating more. And as for my uncle having told Belinda not to speak to you, you should make a complaint to your mother. I do not think she made the agreement which she did to see you nearly as shut off from my cousin as you were before."

Fitz considered this rebuke in silence, leaving Kate to reflect on the source of her own unhappiness. It had to do, she knew, with her encounter with Dev the night before, an encounter she had found immensely upsetting, although she was not certain why. It might be that she felt a certain humiliation because of the easy way he had treated her toward the end of the conversation, but she thought it was something more. Certainly, she was not troubled by the fact that he had sat with Sir George and Belinda all evening, pretending to nurse a lame leg. She was glad he had made such a clever arrangement, and thus kept her cousin from the mincing performance Sir George had planned. And if it had been part of his kindness to keep her uncle and her cousin laughing all evening, why, she was glad to see them amused and happy.

Perhaps, Kate thought, watching a drop of rain weave an uncertain course down the window, her discomfort came from the fact that she felt a certain embarrassment in letting Dev know that she had actually sent a servant to find out what was the worst scandal being circulated about him. Granted that she had done it for a reason. After all, he had told her that he intended to set Sir George off his course by appearing to have damaged his reputation in an unpardonable manner. But somehow she felt that she had gone further than he had expected her to, and as a consequence made herself vulnerable in a way she could only feel and not comprehend. It was as though she had made herself one of that group of simpering, giggling ladies who surrounded him and his friends whenever they came into a room.

Well then, she decided, the only answer for it was to remove herself as far as possible from his affairs at once. Belinda must stand on her own two feet and protest whatever fresh insanity her father had in mind. Perhaps she would be lucky enough not to have to do so, for last night, when they had returned in the carriage, Sir George seemed to consider the match a certainty, and had all but admitted that 'Dev' seemed to like Belinda very well, just as she was. Yes, that was the way it should work out, Kate decided. Sir George would let his daughter alone to be herself, and then discover something about the young marquess which he could not forgive.

A deep sigh from Fitz distracted Kate from her reflections, and she glanced up to see him looking the very picture of despair. A wave of impatience washed over her.

"I dare say you could be making better use of your time than sitting here heaving sighs," she said. "You will forgive me for being frank, sir, but it seems to me that self-pity is the bane of your existence. You say my cousin has written to you? Very well. Have you at least written back? And what sort of letters were they? Did you encourage her to look forward to a future when you will be together? Did you make arrangements for a rendezvous? If you want to win her, you must take advantage of every opportunity."

In response, Fitz stared at Kate for a few minutes, and then declared that it would be a waste of time to exert himself.

"How can you say such a thing, sir?" Kate exclaimed, leaping up from her chair. "How can you simply throw up your hands in such a way?"

Looking her straight in the eyes, Fitz declared that it was quite easy to acknowledge defeat when Lord Gilcrest was, at this very moment, being ushered into the house.

"*He* will be given a proper welcome," Fitz muttered. "*He* will be bowed and scraped to. *He* will be all but offered her hand, whether he wants it or not. If you wish to see the performance, Miss Harrison, you have only to go to the drawing room directly."

"I think you are fantasizing, sir," Kate retorted. "Lord Gilcrest is not expected here today."

Fitz looked at her narrowly. "It may be that he is not expected," he retorted, "but he is here all the same, unless it was his ghost I just saw mount the front stairs."

Automatically, Kate strained to look out the rain-stained windows but of course it was too late. Indeed, it was such a torrent outside that she could not even see to the curb to discover if there was a carriage there. She looked at Fitz with a sort of helplessness which seemed to please him. At least he stopped resting his forehead on his right hand, a pose he often struck when he was feeling most dismal. And then, quite suddenly, Nell had joined them and she was clearly in a flap.

"Sir George is quite beside himself, miss!" she exclaimed. "Lord Gilcrest is here, you see, and has asked to see Miss Belinda. And just think! When he chanced to see me in the hall, he bowed and spoke to me. Called me Miss Robinson, he did, although I cannot think how it was that he remembered. Oh dear, Mr. Ronhugh! I never saw you sitting there in the shadows. What a start you gave me!"

Kate made no attempt to keep the abigail from rambling on. So Dev had called to see Belinda. Was it possible that he had finally found himself attracted by her innocence and quiet ways? Certainly, she must have won his respect, which is more than Kate thought that she had done.

"You *see?*" Fitz muttered. "All Lord Gilcrest has to do is walk in at the door, and Sir George will kill the fatted calf."

"Oh, do stop feeling sorry for yourself!" Kate exclaimed impatiently. "Nell. My cousin does not mean to see him alone, does she?"

"He asked for you as well, miss," the abigail replied, taking two steps toward the door and two steps back in her excitement. "Did I forget to say that? I expect I did. But the main thing is that you must come upstairs at once, because Sir George and Lady Prudence are having such a quarrel that I cannot think what will come of it, and Miss Belinda can only stand there and beg them to stop, which does no good at all."

She had not finished her recital before Kate was out the door. Thankfully, she saw that Tom had had the wit to close the door of the drawing

153

room behind their guest. But even so, there was a danger he might hear what was going on above, for on the stairs Kate could hear nearly every word which Sir George and Lady Prudence exchanged.

"You cannot mean to throw her at that fellow's head!" the baronness cried as Kate reached the landing. "There is no excuse, now that you know what he is!"

"I have told you before that Dev is no better nor no worse than I was as a young man!" Sir George replied angrily. "And may I remind you, ma'am, that Belinda is my daughter, and I will do whatever I think best for her."

"There is nothing 'best' about making her marry a gentleman she does not care for!" Lady Prudence retorted, in an extraordinarily loud voice indeed. "Fancy putting my Fitz in the library and telling Belinda to stay well away from him! As though he were a mad dog, sir! And when the real mad dog arrives, what happens to him? Why, he is received as a favored guest, sir. A favored guest!"

Kate arrived at the top of the stairs, breathless, to see Lady Prudence and her uncle facing one another like pugilists in a ring, with Belinda their only spectator. "Oh, Kate!" she cried when she saw her cousin. "You must do something. This is too dreadful!"

"Uncle!" Kate said. "Recall yourself, do!"

The lace of his cuffs brushed her face as he motioned her away without so much as looking at her. Under the black wig, Sir George's face was a deep shade of purple.

"Lady Prudence!" Kate cried. "Come away, do. Clearly, Uncle is beside himself. I am afraid that he will do some sort of damage."

"It is no fault of mine if your uncle prefers to be—to be a sapskull!" Lady Prudence cried.

"It is none of your *business,* damme!" Sir George exclaimed.

"Ah, but I have made it my business, sir, in the name of two innocents who love one another!"

"Your son is not an innocent, ma'am, he is an ignoramus!"

There was a small vase on a table close at hand, and before Kate could prevent her, Lady Prudence clutched it. There was no knowing what she might have done, had not Kate placed herself bodily between the two and thrown out her arms to make a sort of barricade of herself.

"Enough!" she cried. "Say *pax,* Uncle! Come now. Say it!"

She had prevented quarrels between her younger brothers and sisters at home like this, but she had never thought to command two people older than herself in such a forceful way, red hair streaming, brown eyes glowing.

Sir George clasped his hands behind his back and kicked the floor with his large, buckled shoes. *"Pax,"* he mumbled.

"And Lady Prudence?" Kate continued, reaching out her hand for the vase.

"Oh, if I must—*pax!*" the baroness declared. "But I have no patience with the man, all the

same. Fitz, is that you peering at us from between the bannisters? Come. We are *non gratis*
here at present. But the time will come when a
certain gentleman of my acquaintance will wish
that he had listened to me. Indeed he will! And I
will relish every moment of it when he comes to
make his apologies."

Fourteen

"Thank goodness the woman has taken herself off!" Sir George exclaimed when the door below was heard to shut. "What a nuisance she has made of herself all around. There's no use looking at me that way, Belinda. She has become a perfect pest, and the same might be said for that shiftless younger son of hers. To think that she would dare to challenge me in my own house. And with Dev downstairs in the drawing room, to boot! Damme, he'll think it a havey-cavey thing to be kept waiting like this."

With a little sob, Belinda picked up her skirts and fled down the hall in the direction of her own chamber, while Nell who had been lurking about in the middle distance took after her, petticoats flying.

"I declare I don't know what's going on!" Sir

George exclaimed in exasperation. "There's no pleasing some people, that much I know."

"Not much has been done to please Belinda, Uncle George," Kate said stoutly. "She has been forced to make eyes at a man she does not love, and has just now seen the gentleman she *is* fond of forced out of the house by insults, and his mother with him. Surely you did not expect her to be pleased."

"All that's of no account," Sir George declared, straightening his wig and fussing a bit with his cravat which had come untied in the heat of battle. "Dev is downstairs waiting for her. That's the main thing."

"I believe he asked to see me, too," Kate declared, uneasy lest her uncle, in his enthusiasm, send Belinda to a tête-à-tête of the sort which might do harm to her reputation were it to become known.

"He only wants you there as companion," Sir George told her, taking out his snuff-box. "Damme, if I don't need something to calm my nerves! What was I saying? Oh, yes. This is the way we will proceed. You will go after Belinda and make certain that she is cheerful and looking her very best when you bring her downstairs."

"All of which will be the simplest thing imaginable," Kate murmured to herself.

"Speak up!" her uncle told her. "No matter to repeat, however. My hearing is excellent, as you should know by now, chit. Indeed, I can hear an impertinence several hundred feet away."

"I'm sorry, Uncle," Kate said in a low voice.

"I do not think you are," Sir George said, after a pause. "But we will let it pass for the time. I do not care how difficult or simple it may be, Belinda is to be downstairs in that drawing room within ten minutes. Is that quite clear?"

Kate declared that it was very clear indeed.

"In the meantime," Sir George went on, raising the snuff-laden back of his hand to his nose, "I will undertake to entertain Dev myself. We had a rare, old time last night, you know. Did I tell you . . ."

"I expect we should not keep Lord Gilcrest waiting any longer than is necessary," Kate said crisply.

"Yes, yes. That's true enough," Sir George replied taking a deep sniff of snuff. Both he and Kate waited for the sneezes which were to follow. They came with satisfying heartiness. One, Two. Three. Four.

"Now," Sir George said, tugging down his long waistcoat, "when you and Belinda join us, I will take my leave of you young people. And directly after I have gone, you will make some excuse and slip out of the room as well. Say that you need to fetch a handkerchief. Any excuse will do. Leave them alone for at least half an hour. And mind you do as I say, chit. Remember. I will be watching you. Give him time to propose. That is all that I want."

Was it possible, Kate marveled, that her uncle could possibly believe that Dev had come to offer for his daughter? Or was it she who was playing the fool? Perhaps that was precisely why Dev had come. Whether or not it was true, she saw no recourse but to do as her uncle demanded.

It was one thing, however, for Sir George to say that Belinda should join Lord Gilcrest quickly, and quite another thing, Kate found, to get her cousin to do it. The fact that the marquess was here meant nothing to her, while the quarrel between her father and Fitz's mother meant everything. Finally, in desperation, Kate suggested that if she would only dry her tears and entertain Lord Gilcrest in a suitable manner, her father might be put in such an excellent mood that he would make his truce with Lady Prudence.

It was not much of a promise, but it was enough, particularly since Belinda was in a mood to cling to trifles. With Nell and Kate's assistance, she tidied her demure blue muslin gown and straightened her mobcap. But she was still distracted, and all the way down the stairs kept asking Kate if she thought that Lady Prudence would ever forgive her father for all the rude things he had said.

Tom, the footman, opened the door to the drawing room for them, while Nell hung over the stair-rail above in a state of considerable excitement. Kate herself, had anyone asked her to speak frankly would have had to confess that she felt a degree of suspense. She was not certain what was about to happen, but she knew she would not leave the room unless it was clear that her cousin wanted her to. Such disobedience might mean that her uncle would return her to the country forthwith, but she knew where her duty lay.

Both gentlemen rose as the two young ladies came into the room, and after a few hearty utterances about nothing in particular, Sir George took his leave.

"But you can find me easy enough afterward, my boy," he said, clapping Dev on the shoulder. "In the library across the hall. That's where I'll be. It might be we'll find some reason to break open a bottle of something or other, eh?"

Kate felt something shrivel inside her, and she guessed from Belinda's expression that her cousin felt the same. No doubt Sir George thought that he was being remarkably subtle, but Kate thought that she had never seen a man who walked so flat-footed, no matter how delicate the terrain. However, Dev made no sign that anything out of the way had been said. Instead, he offered Sir George a hearty handshake, and said that nothing would please him more than to share a bottle with him.

But as soon as Sir George had left the room, conspiratorially closing the door behind him with a wink and a nod, the young marquess's mood changed, and he became altogether serious.

"First I must thank both of you ladies for seeing me with no prior notice," he said with so much formality that Kate was startled.

Belinda, still distracted, murmured something, and continued to tear her handkerchief to shreds, but Kate declared in a clear voice that she knew he would not come had it not been important.

"Yes," he said. "Well, the truth is that I have

161

decided that what must be done requires your knowledge and cooperation, Miss Tigford."

And then, before Kate could really believe what she was hearing, he proceeded to outline what had been done to this point: how it had happened that he had realized that Belinda was being put to charm him against her will: how he and Kate with Nell as chaperone had plotted to keep her from embarrassment, and his decision that Sir George could only be dissuaded from having him as son-in-law if he knew something about him of such discredit as to make an alliance impossible. With considerable relief, Kate realized that he intended to say nothing about her contact via Nell with Nanny Benbow. No doubt he thought that it was up to her to tell Belinda that if she saw fit, which was, Kate thought, extraordinarily decent of him.

Belinda's response to the news was first one of bewilderment and disbelief. But when assured by Kate that it was all quite true, and that they had had nothing in mind but her happiness, Belinda began to beam. In fact, she made a little speech in which she thanked them both and then typically sat back in her chair and folded her hands, waiting for someone to make the next proposal.

And this Lord Gilcrest did. It had come to him the night before, he said, that to play Sir George's game meant any amount of trouble.

"Because of your father," he said to Belinda, "neither you nor I could dance all evening. There is no end of bother attendant on the lie. This morning, for instance, when I came into the house,

I quite forgot to limp and only remembered it in time to greet your father. And it will be good fortune if I remember it when I see him later in the library."

Mention of the library brought Belinda to attention. "Since we are being frank," she said, "you may as well know that he thinks you will come to join him with the intention of announcing for me."

"I guessed something of the sort," Lord Gilcrest said with a narrow glance at Kate, as though to make certain the irony did not escape her. "But I shall have to disillusion him, beginning today. And the sooner the process takes place, the less painful it will be for everyone concerned. That is why I have made a plan, a plan which requires the help of both of you."

Kate wondered why his dark eyes avoided her. No doubt it was because of the revelations she had made the night before. She had been audacious in a particular way which had annoyed him. Very well, then. She would help with this plan if it seemed a sensible one. And then she would put him out of her mind, once and for all.

"Miss Harrison was good enough to discover some information which is important to us," Dev was telling Belinda. "You will recall that Lady Ronhugh had a private encounter with your father the other day."

"You told Lord Gilcrest about that?" Belinda asked Kate, clearly bewildered that so much had gone on that she knew nothing of.

"It was to help you," Kate murmured.

163

Suddenly Belinda seemed to come alive. "You told him everything?" she demanded. "About the way Papa was rehearsing me? About Papa's plans? Everything?"

"It—it began quite accidentally," Kate protested. "Lord Gilcrest heard something that I said, that evening that you broke the string of brilliants. And he made a deduction from that which let him guess what your father was doing. I only confirmed what he already knew. When he came here . . ."

"He has been here before?" Belinda exclaimed. "And you said nothing of it to me?"

"I—we only thought you would be distressed," Kate told her.

Never before had she seen Belinda angry. Indeed, she had thought her cousin quite incapable of that particular emotion. But now Kate saw that she had been very wrong. Belinda's face was flushed and her blue eyes glittered like bits of autumn sky.

"I would not have believed it of you!" she exclaimed. "Scheming and plotting with Lord Gilcrest behind my back! Telling him Papa's little plans! It was bad enough that I should have to endure hearing them myself! Did you tell the gentleman that I broke the necklace to attract his attention? No need to answer. It is all too clear that you did."

"But Lord Gilcrest understood," Kate began. "He knows your father and . . ."

"Oh, I expect both of you are very clever in dealing with fools like Papa and I!" Belinda cried.

"I can hear you discussing us! I expect both of you felt so sorry for me! Oh, yes. I see it all now. You told him about Papa's plans for the minuet, did you not? That was why he was conveniently lame and could not dance. And Papa was so pleased to have the great 'Dev' sit with us the entire evening. It did not occur to him that he was being ridiculed! Certainly it did not occur to me! But then I expect you are quite expert at manipulating people, Lord Gilcrest! What an amusing story all this will make when you next see your friends."

Lord Gilcrest rose. His face could have been cut out of marble, Kate thought. She herself felt cold inside. No one had laughed at Belinda, true, but she could imagine how humiliating her cousin found it to discover that other people had discussed her behind her back, made plans to deal with her situation.

"We should have told you at the start, Miss Tigford," the young marquess said in a low voice. "What can I say except to express a hope that you can forgive us?"

It was so exactly what Kate wanted to say herself that she was startled into exclaiming her agreement. "Yes, that is it precisely," she said, going to sit beside her cousin on the scarlet and silver striped settee. "It was thoughtless. But there was this, as well. It crossed my mind more than once that you should know, and then I thought of what a dutiful daughter you are and always have been. You could have felt it necessary to tell your father."

Suddenly Belinda turned very pale. She took Kate's hand with icy fingers. "Of course," she said. "Forgive me for bursting out at you that way. I might have told him, particularly at the beginning. There have never been any secrets between us, you see. But now I think . . ."

Kate met Dev's dark eyes with her own. They waited.

"But now I think that I have earned the right to a secret or two," Belinda declared, squeezing Kate's hand. "You say you have a plan, Lord Gilcrest. If it will dissuade my father from pursuing this absurd course, I will take a part in it. It has, I think, something to do with your reputation. Tell me, have I guessed right? I have never been one to scheme, you see, but that does not mean that I am ignorant of the process."

Kate did not blame her cousin for administering this final rebuke. Indeed, she thought that she and Dev had been dealt with more easily than they deserved. Perhaps, she thought, it had been a good thing to have had Sir George press Belinda as he had. Certainly, it had forced her to stand on her own two feet and not to take everything he said and did as certain as night and day. Besides, she liked the air of confidence about her cousin. It gave a color to her character.

"Very well," Dev said. "I will come straight to the point. Since none of the ready scandal about me shocked your father, Miss Tigford, it came to me that I must act one out in front of him. It must be something which he cannot ignore or forgive, something which affects him. And that is

166

why it must have to do with you. But, mark me, I will attempt nothing without your approval. And yours, Miss Harrison, since you are involved, as well. And now, if you will listen to me closely . . ."

Fifteen

Lord Gilcrest's suggestion that they make up a party to Vauxhall on the following evening helped somewhat to compensate for Sir George's disappointment that 'that young scoundrel, Dev' had not offered for Belinda. True, he cast the blame for that on Kate who had not left the couple together as he had told her to do.

"You knew full well I wanted to give them a little time alone," he had grumbled after Lord Gilcrest had left and Belinda was upstairs. "These things must be done properly. No one knows that better than Dev. He needed the chance to woo her a bit. Steal a kiss or two, perhaps. There is nothing wrong with that, surely, when a gentleman's intentions are honorable."

Kate murmured something to the effect that

she was sorry, but Sir George was too busy with his complaint to listen to her.

"Dash it, gel, what possessed you to stay?" he demanded. "All that needed doing was for you to slip out, and Dev would have taken care of the rest."

Kate searched about for an answer and finally murmured something about not feeling that it was quite proper to leave them alone.

"If I think it is proper, damme, then it is!" Sir George declared. "Well, well! I'm not about to lose my temper with everything going along in such a fine fashion. Vauxhall is a gay enough place for anyone. The sort of spot to fit Dev to a *T*. He'll romance her there, I'll be bound! And I will be on hand to see that you give him a chance to do it, young lady."

Kate agreed, although it made her feel guilty to know in advance just how wrong her uncle was. Surely, it was cruel to raise his hopes so high, and then dash them to the ground. She had mentioned this to Dev, but he had reminded her in turn that her uncle was prepared to separate his only daughter from the gentleman she really loved in order to satisfy his own ambition.

"It will not do, you know," he said and Belinda had supported him.

"I hate to disappoint Papa," she said. "You know I never want to see him unhappy, Kate. But I must either disappoint him now, knowing that he will get over it in time, or stand by and let him drive Fitz away completely."

And so Kate took her scolding patiently, and

listened to Sir George's plans for the following evening. And then she went upstairs and told Belinda what he had said, with Nell sitting on the footstool between them in a way which had become her habit, listening intently. It only followed, as a consequence, that she had to be told something of the plan.

"La!" she exclaimed when Kate and Belinda had finished their recitation. "I wonder that you agreed to it, either one of you. Fancy your letting yourself be jilted, Miss Belinda, and I would not think you would want to play the flirt, Miss Kate. Why, whatever will other people think?"

"That is why Lord Gilcrest chose Vauxhall Gardens as the place to do it, Nell," Belinda said earnestly. "They say there are such crowds about, particularly of an evening when a concert is being played in the pavilion or fireworks are planned, that no one notices anything except the entertainment."

Whereupon the abigail declared that she would give the world to go with them, and said that she would propose just such an expedition to Tom if it were not for the fact that entry was an expense. All of which was followed by reflections on the way the gentry kept the best things for themselves, whereupon she remembered where she was and with whom, and pink with embarrassment left the room.

"Perhaps it is no kindness to make such a friend of her," Kate mused. "But, strangely enough, ever since the day she was Miss Robinson and my companion—you know, the day Lord

Gilcrest came and you were not here—I find it hard to think of her as an abigail. Indeed, it does seem not right that we should go out and about every day and night without counting the cost, and she cannot even go to Vauxhall."

It did not take much further musing on the topic before it was decided that, a tip surely being well in order considering the help Nell had been to them, she and Tom would go after all. And then, having taken care of every incidental including the choosing of the gowns they were to wear, they found their way back to the only subject which truly occupied their minds, both agreeing that surely the plan could not fail.

"And I think Lord Gilcrest was quite right not to go into detail as to what he precisely intends to do," Belinda declared. "It must not seem as though we were acting. When he turns his attention to you, it must take me by surprise. At least the timing of it must, and the particular way he does it. Tell me, Kate, should I seem disappointed?"

"If it had really happened, would you be?"

Belinda shook her mobcapped head. "Goodness, you know I would be relieved," she said.

"Then that is what you must be when it happens," Kate declared. "Your father will sense that something is wrong if you appear to be hurt, I think. He knows how you feel about Fitz, after all."

"Do you think Papa will be angry with you?" Belinda wanted to know next. "I do not like to think that might be the case."

"Lord Gilcrest seemed to think that if I make no effort at all to flirt, and he is the one to make every move, that your father will have no cause to be annoyed with me," Kate reminded her. "Still, I think I will be prepared for annoyance, at the very least."

"But the main thing is that he should be so furious with Lord Gilcrest that he will forget his Grand Design," Belinda said in a low voice. "Oh, it is a clever plan."

"I expect Lord Gilcrest has made many clever plans before this," Kate said dryly. "No doubt your father is not the first one he has deceived, one way or another."

"That is not very kind of you," Belinda said. "I think Lord Gilcrest has gone to a good deal of trouble and I am grateful to him. Why, did you not hear him say that it may well be that this may convince Papa that he is not a good judge of character, in which event he will not force me on some other gentleman whose title and fortune are to his liking?"

At that, Kate had had no choice but to admit that Lord Gilcrest had been singularly thoughtful, but inside she seethed. How right she was to think that she had lost his respect when she had sent Nell to Nanny Benbow to find out scandal about him. From that moment on he had considered her as a lady without scruples. How ironic it was that he had thought her something she was not when he had first met her, and had come to do the same now. Well, she had not enlightened him with the truth there in the autumn-yellow meadow when she had helped him to the doctor, and she would not do so now. The proof of his opinion of her rested in the easy way he had proposed that she should become the presumed new focus of his attention. She remembered the pains he had taken to persuade Belinda to play her part, but he had simply assumed that Kate would join them in the scheme. No doubt he thought her as lacking in character as the ladies with whom he surrounded himself, Kate thought bitterly, but without their sophistication. Gauche and full of guile, not a particularly pleasing combination.

And so she continued to fume quietly to herself during the hours which separated them from Vauxhall, suffering in silence the meals during which her uncle did nothing but boast of Belinda's conquest, listening to Nell's excited commentary about her and Tom's plans to go to the pleasure garden on the same night as 'the master,' now that they were in funds, and quieting Belinda's fears that Lady Prudence had been so offended that neither she nor her youngest son would ever step foot in the house again.

Finally the time had come, and although Belinda seemed quite calm, too much distracted perhaps by the fact that neither Lady Prudence nor Fitz had been seen or heard from, Kate's nerves were not being at all kind to her. But as she donned the green and white striped gown which was her favorite, and puffed out petticoats and all the lace which trimmed bodice and sleeves, she found herself a prey to a strange anxiety. And as she set the broad-brimmed hat with the green silk crown on her red curls, she asked herself if what she was really afraid of had to do with Belinda at all. Perhaps if she were honest with herself she might admit that she was looking beyond this evening's jaunt to Vauxhall. If Dev's plan was successful, Sir George would return home waxing wrathful and determined that 'Dev,' who would no doubt have turned miraculously into 'Lord Gilcrest,' would never darken his door again.

Was that, Kate asked herself, precisely what she wanted? Why had it not occurred to her before that if Dev were to prove himself unworthy to be a suitor to Belinda, he would be beyond the pale entirely. Belinda must not have anymore to do with him, and the same rule would extend to herself. And she could never ever tell her uncle that it was all pretense. The ban against Dev would stand. "Obey your uncle," her father had told her when she left for London, and of course she must.

But as she took a last glance at herself in the pier glass, Kate told herself that it did not matter. Dev would not want to see any more of any of them, once he had accomplished this particular coup, a coup arranged out of kindness in part, and also, Kate thought, because he was as fond of Sir George of winning games.

Belinda joined her, a picture in blue silk, her golden hair lightly dusted with powder and the

175

broad blue ribbon which held her hat in place tied jauntily under her chin. Indeed, she was in good spirits, having decided, as she told Kate in a whisper, to make an active pursuit of Fitz once this affair with Lord Gilcrest was over.

"Papa has taught me the virtues of boldness," she said with a little smile, "and I think it would be a pity not to practice such an admirable art. Don't you agree?"

And Kate agreed. In her present mood she thought she might well have agreed to anything. When Nell darted into her bedchamber just before they left in order to show how smart she looked in the pale pink muslin gown which Belinda had given from her own wardrobe, together with a fine straw hat, Kate had been lavish with her compliments, determined to display an ease of manner she was very far from feeling.

Dev called for them in his phaeton, as he had promised he would do, promptly at eight and they set off toward the river at a spanking clip with their host as driver. Sir George was in the greatest good humor, going on at a great rate about feeling scarcely more than a boy tonight, and so much other nonsense that Kate did not listen to him. But when he swore a great oath and half turned in his seat, Kate gave him her attention.

"Damme, if that wasn't Lady Prudence and those sons of hers!" he declared. "I saw that young cub who is always around the house tip his hat to you, Belinda. I thought I told you not to encourage him."

He spoke in a hoarse whisper, no doubt to keep his precious Dev from hearing, Kate reflected. She did not understand the precise cause of the hostility that was rising in her, but it seemed to be sending its tendrils out in every direction, so that everyone about her caused irritation. She could even be impatient with Lady Prudence for having made her appearance at this particular moment.

It was a pleasant spring evening with the sun dissolving into molten gold and the streets crowded with pleasure-seekers in carriages of all description. Lady Prudence's hired equipage was a good deal shabbier than most, and as a consequence easy to distinguish. As Belinda protested that she had not encouraged Fitz to tip his hat and Dev turned his attention to the traffic. Kate noted that Harry was turning Lady Prudence's carriage about with great alacrity, and that it appeared that she meant to follow them.

Fortunately Sir George was seated so that he could not see, as was Belinda, and it was left to Kate to keep her peace as they rolled down toward Vauxhall with Lady Prudence and her four sons in direct pursuit. Kate dared not anticipate what would happen next. Perhaps the baronness only wanted to know where they were going out of curiosity's sake. Or perhaps she meant to accost Sir George and ask him to apologize for what he had said to her. Kate could only hope that curiosity alone was the answer, and that once it was satisfied Lady Prudence and her sons would rattle away to wherever it was that they had originally been going.

Suddenly, she saw the gardens and she caught her breath, forgetting Lady Prudence in her wonder at the lights that were already sparkling in the growing dusk. Belinda was delighted, too, and all haste was made to see the horse and carriage taken care of and entry made into the famous gardens beside the Thames.

Even in the country, Vauxhall Gardens was spoken of as being one of the sights of London which must be seen, and Kate's own father had told her of his delight at first being taken there as a child. There was a beautiful pavilion, he said, with a curved stage facing the gardens from which famous singers entertained the crowds. And also facing outward, in the same building, were alcoves shaped and decorated like Moorish windows where tables and benches had been set and people feasted. And everywhere there were graceful trees and shrubs and flowers and sheltered walks. It had been at the point of the sheltered walks that he had broken off, seemingly a bit disconcerted, and Kate had had to take recourse to her older brother to discover that the gardens were a favorite trysting place for lovers. Now she found herself wondering if those same walks were to play any part in whatever it was that Dev had planned.

But the crush was too great for much reflection, Kate found. It was worse by far than Almack's, for beside the familiar faces of members of the *haut ton* with their flow of lace and drooping

178

feathers and elaborate wigs, there were staid members of the middle class, squires up from the country with their sturdy wives and merchants from the city itself. And that was not the end of the social mix, for Kate noted not a few shifty-eyed fellows whom she thought might very likely be pickpockets for a profession, not to mention a plentitude of ladies sporting so much vermilion on their faces that they might well have been stricken by a fever.

Into this democratic concoction, Sir George plunged with enthusiasm with Kate clinging to his arm, thus leaving Belinda and Lord Gilcrest to follow.

"Come along, my dear," Sir George muttered. "With any luck we will lose them directly in the crowd. By the end of the evening, the business should be done, eh? A little wine. The pretty lights. And music, too. Oh, Dev is no fool. He must have known how easily he could be alone with Belinda here to mix a little adventure and romance. A heady mixture ... What ho! Why, they are directly behind us. The nuisance of it! And all because you walk so slowly. Here, let us try once more!"

And with that he sped along the gravel path at such an extraordinary speed that Kate was nearly lifted from the ground. Indeed, she was soon forced to run to keep up with his long strides, and when at last he came to a stop his face was moist and scarlet from the exertion he had made. Nothing could have proved more disconcerting to him, as a consequence, than to turn and find Lord Gilcrest and Belinda directly behind him.

Had it not been that Kate was breathless, she would have had to laugh. But as it was, she and Belinda both pleaded exhaustion, and soon were settled at one of the tables beneath the trees with Sir George tugging at his wig and muttering to himself, clearly bewildered that Dev had not taken advantage of such an obvious opportunity to be alone with his daughter.

Until now Kate had not looked directly at Dev all evening. But now she found herself seated across from him, and it was impossible not to meet his eyes. Even though she knew they were conspirators, she drew a deep breath when he winked at her, a slow wink of amusement. The irritation which she had felt before returned in full strength. True, they had agreed to cooperate with him, both herself and Belinda. But that did not give him carte blanche to be familiar with either one of them.

A waiter appeared, and Sir George ordered wine with the hopeful manner of one who never allows himself to be completely crushed. But when it came, it was he who drank most deeply, Kate noticed, and Dev who restrained. No doubt, she thought, the younger man wanted to keep his head quite clear for the manipulations which, she assumed, were to follow. Until now he had showed no particular attention to her, and if he did not commence at once she feared that her uncle might be too soothed by the wine to notice anything except the gravest possible indiscretions on Dev's part. And then, quite suddenly, it began.

"My dear Miss Harrison," Dev said warmly. "Will you permit me to tell you that I have never seen you look as lovely as you do tonight?"

Kate held her breath, fearing an outburst from her uncle at that. But when she looked at him it was to find him staring apoplectically at the table directly across from them where Lady Prudence sat with her four sons.

Sixteen

At the same moment in which Sir George made his discovery, a high-bosomed lady stepped onto the bow-fronted stage which jutted from the pavilion and held out a musical score. It was a brilliant scene, with the lamps set in glass globes above the stage glittering on the singer's bejeweled hair and throat. Behind her the musicians in their tri-cornered hats raised their instruments. People flocked about from every quarter of the gardens and the singer's rich, contralto voice filled the warm spring air.

"That is the famous Mrs. Weichsel," Dev declared, addressing himself exclusively to Kate, his voice intimate and low. "Have you ever heard her sing before, my dear Miss Harrison?"

Kate glanced at her uncle to see if he were listening, and found that he was still staring balefully at Lady Prudence and her sons and muttering under his breath. As for Belinda, she seemed to have forgotten the drama they were supposed to be acting out for her father's benefit, for her eyes, too, were trained on the group opposite.

Dev shrugged his shoulders helplessly and Kate shook her head, both mute messages indicating that it was clearly no use proceeding while Sir George was so distracted. Even a casual passer-by might have thrown the baroness's party more than a passing glance if for no other reason than that Lady Prudence's bulbous eyes and Roman nose had been bequeathed in diminishing dimension to Frederick, Frank, Fairbanks and Fitz in precisely that order, so that to see them sitting in close proximity to one another was like seeing the same image reduced four times. To make the sight of them even more unusual, mother and sons shared a common expression of watchful antagonism which was centered exactly on Sir George.

"This won't do!" the object of their attention muttered. "This won't do at all! There. I'll take another glass of wine to bolster myself and then I'll have a word with her ladyship. See if I don't. I won't be followed about like a sapskull, indeed I won't!"

"But this is a public garden, Papa," Belinda protested. "They have a perfect right to be here."

"Damme if they do!" Sir George declared so loudly that it blended with the voice of Mrs.

Weichsel, and several members of her audience raised the cry of 'Hush!' and 'Shame!'

Disregarding them completely, Sir George rose to his feet, his shoulders raised belligerently. Following his example, the four sons of Lady Prudence rose as well. And when Sir George took a few steps toward them, they did the same, although Fitz remained a bit behind, his face twisted into an expression of unbearable gloom.

And then, quite suddenly, Lady Prudence took command of the situation. While the contralto wailed and wabbled her way up a scale and down the other side, Lady Prudence rapped the table with her fan, whereupon, as on command, the four young men turned back and rejoined her.

"I should do the same, Papa," Belinda urged. "Oh, do sit down and listen to the music. Lady Prudence only means to take her revenge for the way you treated her the other day by making you uncomfortable. Only let her see you do not mind, she will grow tired of it."

The vocalist came to the end of her song with a merry 'Tra la la,' and the crowd applauded enthusiastically. Sir George, meanwhile, appeared to consider, and then returned to the table.

"Those young ruffians mean to threaten me," he grumbled, re-addressing himself to the wine.

"Fitz is not a ruffian, Papa, and neither are his brothers. It was the way you approached them that was at fault. No doubt Lady Prudence told them how you treated her and—and they feel she needs protection."

"Damme, what's wrong with you, gel?" Sir

George retorted. "Making me appear to be in the wrong! I won't have it, you know."

Dev and Kate exchanged another glance. Clearly, they had been forgotten.

"But, Papa, I was only trying to explain," Belinda cried. "Come. If they are going to upset you, we can move to another table."

"At this time of the evening they are certain to be taken," Dev interposed. "We were lucky to get one as it is."

"Wouldn't move if there were a hundred tables waiting," Sir George declared defiantly. "No intention of letting that woman trouble me. Pity her poor husband, that's the only thing. Well, now, what were we about? Oh, yes. The wine."

And pouring himself another glass, Sir George began to rub his hands and go through all the pantomime of a self-satisfied man, a display which was clearly put on for Lady Prudence's benefit. He meant, Kate thought, to show the baronness that Belinda was quite settled, and thus to dampen her hopes forever. It was an irony, Kate thought, that if Dev carried through with what he planned Lady Prudence's ambitions would be rekindled, instead.

Mrs. Weichsel had disappeared from the platform now, and the musicians were playing a lilting tune. Ladies preened themselves as they promenaded, and laughter filled the warm night air. In the midst of such a scene, Sir George's stilted attempt to be the heart and soul of merriment struck a discordant note.

"I wonder, sir," Dev said in one of those rare

186

intervals when Sir George had paused for breath, "if you mind very much were your niece and I . . ."

Kate assumed that he was about to propose that they take a walk together, but this attempt to outrage her uncle was doomed to failure as he continued to talk. Indeed, he was a perfect convulsion of activity as he gestured broadly with his left hand, raised his wineglass with his right, and paused to pound on the table with both fists to attract the attention of a waiter when the bottle was empty.

Having never seen her uncle act with anything other than perfect decorum when he was in public, Kate was amazed, and it was clear from the expression on poor Belinda's face that she was in the throes of acute embarrassment. Across the way, Lady Prudence and three of her sons watched the proceedings with considerable interest, while Fitz contented himself with scowling at the middle distance, and looking quite as miserable as it was possible to look in a place of public entertainment.

Dev and Kate exchanged glances and raised their eyebrows, but beyond that there seemed little that they could do. Clearly Sir George had been so recalled to the days of his reckless youth, either by Vauxhall Gardens at night, the companionship of a 'gay young rake' like Dev, or a combination of both.

"Did ever anyone have so many reasons to celebrate?" her uncle was demanding now, raising his glass and swinging it in such a broad arc that some of the passers-by clearly thought they had been included in a toast, and raised their hats to him.

"Oh, we are very fortunate, Papa," Belinda said in a small voice. "But there is no need to make such a hue and cry about it, surely."

"The ladies will exaggerate," Sir George chuckled, with a conspiratorial smile in Dev's direction. "I expect you have often found that to be the case, my boy. Oh, there's many a fine story we could tell one another, I'll be bound. Just men together on either side of a fireplace, eh? Well, there'll be a time for that when the wooing's over!"

"Papa!" Belinda hissed in a scandalized tone.

"I think we will have to reconsider our plan for the time being," Dev muttered to Kate when the waiter arrived with more wine. "I can gauge your uncle's temper in the ordinary way of things. But when a man is in his cups, there is no way of telling what he will do and when."

"Ah, yes," Sir George was muttering to himself, resting his chin on his waistcoat, "when the wooing's done . . ."

"Can you do nothing to stop him?" Belinda demanded in a whisper. "He is making a scandal of himself!"

"Perhaps, sir, if we were to walk . . ." Dev began, rising to his feet.

But Sir George did not seem able to focus his attention as he should. "Damme, but you're a handsome fellow, Dev my friend," he declared. "And I'll be dashed if you don't wear your clothes with as much of a dash as I did when I was a young scamp. Mark you, waistcoats were longer then, and I wore my cuffs turned back to my elbow. But times change. Times change."

He closed his eyes and gave every appearance of being about to drift into a sound sleep despite the fact that he was sitting bolt upright, and Kate felt a moment's pity for him. What had he done, after all, but try to use Belinda to help him to recapture the past? No doubt, in the dreams which were rising up about his mind together with the fumes of the claret that he had drunk, he saw himself much as Dev appeared now—broad-shouldered and handsome and with that vague hint of arrogance about his manner which distinguished him and his friends. But those were dreams. The truth told of a stout and aging personage who wore his waistcoats rather too long for current fashion, and was, at this precise moment, beginning to snore so loudly that the musicians raised their eyes from the music and looked about rather wildly as though they had just heard a misplaced bassoon.

Belinda, scarlet with embarrassment now, glanced across the way to where Lady Prudence and her sons sat about a table. Following her cousin's eyes, Kate saw that the baroness looked amused and that Frederick, Frank, and Fairbanks imitated her expression, while Fitz glowered at the scene.

"Oh dear, I did not think that she could be so cruel!" Belinda exclaimed.

"Her quarrel is not with you but with your father," Kate said quickly. "You must not take anything she does in that regard personally. Your father would have been just as amused had the situation been reversed. You must admit that."

"Oh, I admit it," Belinda wailed. "But that does not make me feel any better. You were good enough to bring us here, Lord Gilcrest. You meant to take the time and effort to relieve me of Papa's scheming. And look what it has come to! You have wasted your time, sir!"

"You must not endow Lord Gilcrest with more altruism than he has a right to claim," Kate said crisply, thinking that it was bad enough to see her uncle humiliated, and that she would not have Belinda demean herself with apologies. "I expect that he would be the first to admit that he would not be here if it did not amuse him to be."

"I see that you are an astute judge of character, Miss Harrison," Dev declared with a smile.

"I do not claim to be," Kate replied. "But I think I am right in this regard."

The flares and candles which were everywhere made the pleasure gardens almost as light as day, but there were still unexpected shadows and some of these seemed to gather on Dev's face as Kate delivered herself of her opinion.

"But of course I am here in search of amusement, Miss Harrison," Dev said. "What other reason does a gentleman like myself have for doing anything?"

"I—I think you are being kind," Belinda said, trying to catch the tear which was wandering down her cheek in a handkerchief.

At that moment Kate heard an exclamation,

and looking over her shoulder once again saw Fitz leap to his feet. For a moment, he bent over the table making a statement of some sort. And then he straightened, and with arms akimbo, waited as his mother and his brothers made a hasty departure without so much as one last smile thrown in the direction of the slumbering Sir George.

"The worm has turned, I think," Kate heard Dev mutter in a voice so low she could not think he meant either her or Belinda to hear. And it was true that her cousin was aware of nothing except the fact that Fitz was crossing the path which had separated the two tables, with nothing but his scowl to make him seem otherwise than a presentable gentleman, properly dressed out in wig and waistcoat with the proper amount of lace at his throat and cuffs. As though drawn upward by a magnet, Belinda rose to her feet.

"I think it might be politic for us to leave them alone," Dev said in a low voice. "In his present condition your uncle is certain not to bother them. Do you agree, Miss Harrison? Will you stroll around a bit with me, or are you afraid your reputation might be ruined?"

"I think you overestimate yourself as a scoundrel, sir," Kate retorted. "What sort of man-about-town is it who must convince someone that he is reprehensible?"

She rose and took his arm. "But that is your concern, sir. I should make no comment on it. We are here together to act out a scene or two only to find that our audience has preferred a deep sleep.

It makes an awkward situation, but perhaps you do not feel it."

"My dear Miss Harrison," he replied. "What reason have I given you for adopting such a cutting manner? I declare that you seemed affable enough, when together with your cousin we evolved this plan."

"We did not evolve it," Kate reminded him. "You presented it to us and we agreed."

"And you are sorry for that now?" he asked her.

Kate did not answer him at once. It suddenly bore in on her that he had chosen a path which appeared to lead away from the general concourse of activity, and that the shrubs which lined the gravel ribbon were so high as to close out a great deal of the light. Furthermore, in the distance, she heard the sudden rise of a lady's laughter on a particular note which could leave no question as to what had occasioned it.

"I think you are too certain of yourself, sir," she announced, pausing in her tracks. "You take it quite for granted that my uncle should want you for his son-in-law. You show your social virtuosity by handling the situation Sir George presented you with so carefully that my cousin's feelings are saved. And you arrange this outing as a final proof that you can manipulate everything. Now that circumstances have provided difficulties for you, you decide to get what little amusement you can from the evening by taking me for a stroll in what must be the darkest part of the gardens, and I warrant not a place decent women are often seen."

"I confess to admitting that we have walked too far from the lights," Dev said after a pause. "You must be pleased to find your poor opinion of me so readily confirmed, Miss Harrison."

It was too dark to see his face, to know precisely where he was. Kate had kept her hand on his arm until she had begun to speak, and then as she fired her own temper she had released him. Now she realized with distress that she could never find her way back on her own. Certainly it would not do to be running about in a place like this with no sure knowledge of direction.

"You condescend, sir," she said as one who has the final word. "And now, I think, we should . . ."

"You are very fond of putting people in their place, Miss Harrison," she heard Dev say. "Your judgments come thick and fast. Tell me, why do you think I chose this path? Certainly, it could not be that I had certain thoughts which occupied my mind and made the choice of where we walked a chance."

"I do not know, I'm sure, sir," Kate said as he took her elbow and guided her along so quickly that she saw the lights and heard the music almost at once.

"I expect that you know full well that to put some small excitement in the evening, I proposed to attack you in the shadows," he went on dryly.

Kate felt her cheeks go hot. "It would fit the sort of character you assume!" she said angrily. "What a story it was to tell me that you wanted to be another sort of person, to start fresh in Virginia, too . . ."

In her fury at being mocked, she had spoke without thinking, and when she stopped it was too late.

"But when could I have ever told you that?" Dev demanded, his hand closing on her arm. "I went to Virginia four years ago and we have known one another no more than weeks. Come, I will not let you slip away until you have explained it to me."

But despite the determination with which he spoke, Kate slipped free and hurried away from him. Her heart was pounding as though she had run a race and she felt as though she would like to cry. But whether, if she did, her tears would be born of rage or disappointment or humiliation, she was not certain.

Seventeen

The next morning the promise of summer was so heavy on the air that the windows of the breakfast room were opened early, and when Kate came downstairs she found the lure of the tiny garden too much to resist. She had often yearned for the country since she had come to London, but never so much as now with the painful experience of the night before still so fresh in her mind.

She was still not certain how much her uncle had guessed about what had happened while he 'napped.' When she had turned the corner of the pavilion and seen that he was awake and in the company of Nell and Tom, Kate had paused and found that Dev was right behind her. For a moment they looked at one another, but neither spoke. Nothing about them had changed. Lights still glowed like fireflies and the orchestra still played. Ladies and gentleman promenaded and waiters dashed hither and thither. Nothing had changed in one sense, and in another, everything was so different that Kate felt lost. What was she doing here? she asked herself. Surely it was not where she belonged.

That was as close as she had allowed herself, then or now, to think of what had happened between her and Dev. Better to concentrate on what had happened subsequently, the way he had held out his arm and murmured something that she did not catch except for the word 'salvage.' They had advanced on Sir George's table slowly, allowing him ample time to see them, for it was certain that his head had not completely cleared as yet, and there was a great rubbing of eyes and looking about in a bewildered sort of way while Tom hovered over him and Nell appeared to shake her head.

"La! I'm that glad to see you, miss," the abigail cried when she caught sight of Kate. "Indeed I don't know what is going on, and that's the truth. Tom and me comes along and sees the master sleeping as sound as though he was in his bed. And Miss Belinda and Mr. Ronhugh talking away to beat the band. And when they see us, Mr. Ronhugh motions to us. La, what good spirit he was in, for though he didn't smile, which was, as I said to Tom, more than could be expected, he didn't scowl so much as usual. And he said that Sir George had had a bit too much wine. Fancy! And that he and Miss Belinda didn't care to leave

196

him alone while they took a promenade. So of course Tom offered to watch the master, but that was thinking that he would still be asleep when they returned. Which turned out not to be the case, miss, and now he wants to know where Miss Belinda is and, oh dear, I think there may be a great fuss!"

But, as it happened, Sir George's head was still too befumed by the claret to allow him to entertain any other emotion but confusion. There had been a good deal of 'What's all this?' and 'Damme' this and that, but he had made no comment on the fact that Kate appeared to have been walking with the very gentleman whom he had chosen for his daughter, and that his daughter—for Belinda and Fitz returned shortly—had been for a promenade with a gentleman he had told her to pay no attention to.

It had taken the combined effort of Tom and Fitz and Dev to assist Sir George to the carriage where, once ensconced, he had settled back to sleep again. Now, looking back through the open French doors to the breakfast room, Kate told herself that it was extremely doubtful that her uncle would choose to make a morning meal today.

But she was wrong. Not ten minutes later, when Kate was buttering herself a piece of bread and waiting for her tea to cool, Sir George came striding into the morning room with all his customary bustle. Indeed, if one had not looked carefully at his eyes and did not know that he was not customarily so pale, it would have been impossible to guess that he must surely be feeling a far cry from top form.

"Ah Kate," he said without smiling. "I wanted to talk to you, dashed if I didn't. And Belinda, too. Nell is to have her down here in ten minutes, if not before. There is a certain matter which we must lose no time in discussing, I believe."

Whatever this matter was, it was clear he had no intention of divulging it to Kate until Belinda had joined them, for he made a great point of occupying himself with his breakfast which was to consist, apparently, of the consumption of great quantities of water, with the little maid who waited on them being sent back twice to fill the pitcher.

"Deuced unseasonable heat gives me a thirst," was all the explanation that he cared to give, and Kate pretended to give no notice. Certainly, if he preferred to make no reference to his condition the night before, that was his privilege.

When Belinda came into the room a few minutes later, she was greeted by silence, Kate thinking it the better part of wisdom not to interfere in any way with whatever it was her uncle meant to do or say. The water seemed to have revived him slightly, but his expression seemed to hint at an uneven disposition at best.

Sir George waited until Belinda had poured her tea before he spoke. "I believe," he said, "that after what happened last night, a few explanations are in order."

"Oh, Papa!" Belinda cried in apparent relief. "We understand. We truly do! It is simply that you have no head for claret. Anyone could have made the same mistake. And after all, what harm did it do? You had a little sleep and were quite recovered, and if Lady Prudence ever makes any reference to your condition, Fitz has assured me that he will speak to her quite sharply. He *can*, you know. Speak sharply to her, I mean. Why, I cannot just recall whether you were still awake last night when . . ."

"Enough!" her father bellowed. "Enough, chit! Did you imagine that I was going to compose some fiction to give me a reason to explain it away? My condition, you say! Why, I should like to know what you mean, damme if I would not! I may have fallen into a nap at some time or another, but that had nothing to do with claret I'll have you know. You have never seen me in my cups, gel, and do you know the reason for it? It is because I have a strong head, miss. None stronger. I should like to see the man who could drink me under the table. Indeed I should! And you speak of my condition!"

His face had grown so scarlet that Kate grew quite worried for him and quickly made an interruption. "Your daughter is so little accustomed to the ways of the world, sir," she said quickly, "that she will make these little errors from time to time. No one else thought anything of it, Uncle, you can be certain of it. Indeed, the music was so delightful that I nearly drifted off myself several times."

She had thought to pacify him, but the exact reverse seemed to be true as he turned toward her, the veins bulging in his cheeks, and thumped the table with both fists.

"*Nearly* drifted away, miss!" he exclaimed. "*Nearly* drifted away! Why, that's a pretty way of saying it, I grant you. No doubt you thought me in such a state that I would never notice. I may have closed my eyes for a minute, miss, but I opened them again directly. Just in time to see *you* 'drifting' away with that damned young scoundrel, eh? I did not care to speak of it last night. Indeed, I think I may have eaten something to put me off, for I did not feel at all the thing. So I decided to postpone it until the morning. But now I see you thought I took no notice of it because—because of my *condition!*"

"Papa!" Belinda cried, leaping from her chair to come to the defense of her friend. "If Kate went for a stroll with Lord Gilcrest, it was only because she saw that Fitz and I wanted to be alone. You are not to blame her! If will be too unfair if you do!"

"So you confess to it!" her father exclaimed. "Perhaps because I did not mention that deplorable young man, or address myself to him when I awakened from my nap, you thought I did not notice him! But I saw everything, miss. Everything! I did not want to spoil the evening or I would have made a fair fuss, I can tell you."

"I thought you did not speak of it because you felt tired and unwell, Papa," Belinda said with her blue eyes steady. "That is what you said a few minutes ago at least."

"You are being pert, miss!" Sir George bellowed

and now it was his turn to leap to his feet. When enraged like this he seemed to fill the morning room with his wig and waistcoat. Even the buckles on his shoes seemed monstrous, although Kate knew it was her fancy. Still, she felt quite suffocated, although she knew it was absurd. Besides, much as she might like to leave the room, she must remain and defend Belinda from her father's wrath. As for defending herself, she had come to think that that was quite beside the point.

"I am sorry, Papa," Belinda said and one golden curl trailed across the white hollow of her throat as she bent her mobcapped head. "I—I never meant to be rude."

"Humph! I don't expect you did, Child," Sir George replied, raising one hand to his head and sinking back into his chair with a look of misery on his face. And, since at home in the country her father's groom was prone to just such attacks the morning after a night spent drinking at the local inn, and was furthermore loquacious when it came to giving out details of precisely how he felt, Kate thought it was the greater part of kindness to sit very, very quiet, with her head bowed like Belinda, until the banging inside her uncle's skull ceased.

"I only wish that you would not pretend to be fond of this fellow Fitz, my dear," Sir George said at last with a sigh. "I know you only do it because you are not certain of yourself, and want it to appear you are well taken care of when it comes to gentlemen. I mean to say, as long as the chap is at your beck and call, you can find some excuse for remaining in the background. But now I will not let you hide behind some absurd pretence of affection for him, simply because you see that your own cousin has decided to become your rival."

"Rival!" Belinda exclaimed.

"Her rival!" Kate cried in amazement.

Sir George smiled in a wooden manner. "I suppose it is only natural," he said sadly. "You saw your cousin about to walk off with a plum, Kate, and you were jealous. Fond as we are of other people, we can be jealous of them, too. And Dev has a roaming eye. You see, I make no excuses for him. He might be able to resist a pretty face as long as the owner made it clear she was not interested in him. But if in some small ways— and, although you are inexperienced, my dear, I fancy they came naturally to you, unlike my poor Belinda—if, as I say, in some small ways the lady let it be known that she would not protest it he were to draw her into the shrubbery . . ."

"Papa!" Belinda cried. "Really, you must not be so unfair, not to mention unkind! Why, if you only knew the truth of it you would realize that Kate is my dearest friend and that she . . ."

Seeing that her cousin's natural honesty was about to lead her to a confession of Dev's plan, Kate broke in on her with a protest of her own which she hoped would serve as a distraction.

"I assure you, sir," she declared firmly, "that if I were to be jealous of Belinda it would more likely be because of Fitz than of Lord Gilcrest! You may think him very fine, sir, and the 'pink

202

of youth,' or something of the sort, but I say he is too full of himself, sir. Yes, he is proud and arrogant, and I suspect he could be cruel if he wanted. The fact is that he thinks of nothing but himself, and I would not lower myself to so much as blink an eye at him, believe me!"

She finished, breathless, to see Belinda and Sir George staring at her, mouths agape.

"Well, well, my dear," her uncle said in a pacifying manner. "I did not mean to send you into such a scold. Damme, I see that you have a temper to match your hair. And I have never once had reason to guess it before. But let me explain. I do believe you. Who could fail to, since you are so vehement? But the fact is that when I saw you coming from the direction of Love Alley, I could only draw one conclusion."

"Love Alley!" Belinda exclaimed. "Why, where is that, Papa? It sounds so very vulgar that I am certain you must have been mistaken."

"I suspect there is just such a place and that I have been in it," Kate said grimly. "Certainly it was not a compliment to have been taken there. But then, I could not have expected Lord Gilcrest to think of the niceties."

"You fly up in the boughs too quickly, my dear," her uncle said, making a tut-tutting sound and pressing the palm of one hand to his forehead. "Why, when I was a young scoundrel like Dev I often took a young lady to that particular walk, and, 'pon my soul, I did not expect her to be insulted."

Kate shook her head until her red curls flew.

"Uncle, uncle," she declared. "I cannot understand you. One minute you were accusing me of having lured Belinda's beau away, and the next you are telling me I should have been complimented to have been taken down Love Alley by Lord Gilcrest. And I must tell you, lest you have the wrong idea, that we only chanced to stray there because his mind was on something else. At least that is what he told me."

"What a scamp the lad is!" Sir George exclaimed, drinking another glass of water. "What I would not give to be fit as a fiddle again, and twenty-four in the bargain. You would not find a bottle of claret meaning much to me then! Not that it has now, of course. Not in the slightest. I only meant to say that when one is in the way of dissipation as a regular way of life . . . But never mind! Never mind! We must be back to business."

"But Papa," Belinda said. "We had no business except that you were to hector us. And I think you have quite finished that."

"Yes, well . . . My head . . . But I will say this. You gels may have been deceived at what Dev was up to, but I know the old tricks too well to be mistaken. He wants you, Belinda. What happened last night was a certain sign of it."

"Oh dear, Papa!" Belinda cried. "I cannot think what you can mean."

"He has presented you with a rival, Child," Sir George declared, the lace of his cuffs flying as he pointed straight at Kate. "He means to play you off against one another, to be sure. And Kate will understand, that, although I do not mean to discriminate . . ."

"Sir," Kate declared, rising. "I will not play a game of rivals with Belinda or anyone else, for either Lord Gilcrest's amusement or for yours. Indeed, if matters pursue their present course there will be no choice for me but to return at once to the country."

Eighteen

"I would not blame you if you left today," Belinda said in a low voice as they strolled in the garden. White roses peeked from the vine which clambered up the wall behind her, roses no paler than her cheeks. She seemed very vulnerable to Kate, as she paced along the path in her billowing white and yellow gown with traces of tears still lingering on her cheeks.

"No. Hear me out, do," Belinda went on. "What have I done since you came here, Kate, but complain about Papa and yearn for Fitz and not do anything to help myself? And Papa has been a scandal. No, I must say it. I have made too many excuses for him already. I dare say it *has* been difficult for him, being both mother and father to me, particularly during my coming-out. But his behavior has been outrageous. And, I declare, I would defy him, particularly now when he would set us up as rivals if he could. But Kate—I am so afraid that if I do he will never consent to Fitz and I being married."

The late spring sun caressed the warm brick which surrounded them on two sides, and struck sparks of gold in the gray stone of the wall which enclosed the little garden. As it had earlier that morning, the scent of early blooming flowers made Kate long to be at home again. Or, were she to be quite honest with herself, it brought a sense of happiness and pain. It would not be the simple thing she pretended to return home now. There would be ties to cut, ties she was almost unwilling to admit existed, even to herself. And then there was her cousin. Certainly, she could not leave London until matters were settled between her and Fitz. For there must be a way to make Sir George see that the two belonged together. And yet, what was it?

"If I go to Papa and say I will play no more of his games with Lord Gilcrest," Belinda said as though she had read Kate's thoughts, "then the most I can hope for is that he will choose someone else with a title and a fortune and a reputation as a rake, and set me after him. Do you not agree?"

Kate was forced to nod her head. "And if you go so far as to tell him that Lord Gilcrest knows the way you feel, and that we three have actually connived together to make him think badly of the man he has chosen," she said thoughtfully, "he will be angry, and nothing will have changed as far as you and Fitz are concerned."

Belinda paused beside the wooden bench which nestled in the corner which trapped the sun. "Then what is to be done?" she said in a small voice. "Fitz—Fitz wants me to run away with him, you know."

Kate stared at her in amazement, for an elopement was something she had not considered as a possibility, given Belinda's obedient nature and Fitz's apparent endless capacity for being dominated by his mother.

"Did he actually suggest it?" she demanded incredulously.

"I know what you are thinking," Belinda said, with a dimple appearing in both cheeks. "But Fitz is different than you think. At least he could be if he had the chance. Oh, Kate, I will die if Papa will not let me marry him! Tell me that there must be some way to persuade him to forget this mad idea that I must marry Lord Gilcrest!"

There must be a way," Kate repeated grimly, her eyes taking on a faraway expression as she tried to think of one. Even if Dev had had a fair opportunity to put his scheme into action, it would have been doomed to fail. She knew that now that her uncle had laughed away the notion that there had been any harm in Dev taking her to Love Alley. There must be something which would shock him, something he had not indulged in as a young man, something which would be so shameful that Sir George could not forgive it.

But there was no use in thinking of that now,

she told herself, and she felt the blood burn in her face as she remembered some of what she had said to Dev there among the shrubbery. He had not addressed another word to her after they had joined her uncle. Indeed, he had not looked at her during the drive home, and once they had reached the house, Kate had given him no opportunity to snub her further, by taking pains to be out of the carriage before he could offer his hand and inside the door before the others had said good night.

Well, she could not blame him if he were angry, she thought now, turning her face up to the spring sunshine as though for consolation. She had insulted him in such a particular way as to make it impossible for them to be more than acquaintances again. And what a fool she had been to allow herself to be so carried away that she had actually made reference to something he had told her four years ago, when she had been with him in a far different guise. All in all, Kate decided, she had not distinguished herself. Still, it *was* true that he was arrogant. It *was* true that he was amusing himself with the attempt to solve Belinda's problem. And if he had not led her into the shrubbery in order to kiss her ... Well, how was she to know he would be such a gentleman? Besides, no doubt that was not it. He would have tried to kiss her if he had wanted to. But he was doubtless so accustomed to the wiles of sophisticated ladies that he found nothing appealing about a red-haired girl from the country who ...

The thought was so bitter that Kate put an end

to it, and tried to show an interest in the flowers which for once she did not feel. Not more than a moment passed in this endeavor when she became aware of the sound of raised voices, and presently she heard the words coming from the direction of the hallway outside the morning room where the French doors stood open to the day.

"But you must be announced, sir!" If you will only wait in the drawing room . . ."

"Damn you, whelp, get the devil out of my way before I knock you over," was the reply, and Kate clasped her hands to her face as she recognized Dev's voice.

And then she saw Tom being backed into the morning room, and saw that Dev had taken the lapels of the footman's liveried coat in one fist, and that, although Tom was far from being a small man, Dev was shaking him as a cat shakes a mouse.

"Damme, I want to see Miss Harrison!" Dev declared, slurring the words so badly that it was clear that he was in his cups. Indeed, even from a distance, Kate could see that his cravat was in disarray and that his dark hair was tousled. In that same moment Dev caught sight of her.

"There's the young lady I am looking for," he said, tossing Tom aside and proceeding across the room toward the French doors with an unsteady gait which took him as much to either side as forward. "How do, Miss Harrison! How do! Top of the morning. All that sort of rot. Make you a bow, I would, if I thought I could keep my balance."

His condition was so far different from any Kate had ever thought to see him in that she felt frozen with a sort of outrage.

"Cat got your tongue?" Dev demanded. "Who's condescending now, I ask you? Well, you can look down your nose all you like, my friend. You *are* my friend, aren't you? Why, damme, I told you you were, four years ago directly after I kicked you in the mud when you were pulling off my boot."

So he *had* recognized her, then, Kate thought, with a sort of fascinated horror. Very well. It would make a good story for him to tell to his smart friends. She hoped it made them laugh. As for herself she did not feel as though she would ever laugh again.

"I—I do not think you are a gentleman for mentioning it," she said, dodging to pass him, just as he leaned in the same direction to prevent it. "Besides, that was years ago, and . . ."

"Wouldn't be so easy for you to pretend to be a lad now, would it?" Dev demanded, looking at her in such a way as made Kate yearn to slap him. Indeed, she raised her hand to do so, only to have him take her by the wrist.

"Let go of me!" Kate demanded, wrenching her arm back and forth with so much energy that her mobcap fell from her head and a cloud of red curls tumbled down on her shoulders.

"Vixen!" Dev said admiringly. "Dash it, I think this is how I like you best. Struggling. In a fury with me. But it's of no use, my little pretty. You may find fault with my character, but you cannot deny that at least I am stronger physically than you."

Kate flung down her arm and he released her, but still he barred her path. Looking back at the house, Kate saw that they were being well observed. From his bedchamber window, Sir George was surveying the sight of his niece and his favorite 'scamp' struggling in the garden. Tom had apparently alerted him to what was going on, for he stood beside his master in the window. Sir George was gaping like a fish. Indeed, to see him without his wig was to see a balding stranger.

"How dare you come here and cause this disturbance?" Kate demanded. "You are obviously drunk, sir, and unless you calm yourself at once I should not be surprised to find you thrown out of the house."

"There's not a man here strong enough to do so," Dev declared. "Just let them try and see what will come of it. I've come to have a word with you, and that is what I intend to do. As for being in my cups . . ."

"Drunk, sir!" Kate flared. "Say the word straight out unless you are too great a coward to face your true condition. Why, you are a scandal!"

"My dear Miss Harrison!" the marquess said in a loud voice, swaying slightly. "It came to me this morning that I had mistaken you in taking what you said to me at Vauxhall seriously. Damme, if it doesn't clear the head to spend a night drinking at my club now and then. But, as I say, it came to me . . ."

"You see!" Kate said triumphantly. "You spent the night drinking. You admit it!"

"A gentleman never admits anything," he told her with half a smile. "But as I was saying, it came to me that you attacked me as you did because you wanted me to show you a bolder attention than I had. You sought to stir me up, you know. You did, indeed. And I have come here to tell you that you have succeeded."

Sir George was leaning out the window now with a look of disbelief on his face and Kate became aware that there was a crowd of sorts gathered in the morning room. In a single glance, she could see Nell and Belinda and Lady Prudence. And then there was a wizened-faced old personage in the most peculiar, old-fashioned gown, someone Kate had never seen before. And everyone was taking the scene in with no attempt at intervention.

She thought of calling out for help, but perhaps that was absurd, since Dev could not hurt her. Indeed, there was no indication that he was even angry. In fact the fondness with which he was looking at her now made her feel quite ill at ease, and for the second time she tried to dart around him and was prevented as before.

"I have a plan," Dev announced, still speaking as loudly as though she were standing on the other side of the garden from him, and moving in a sort of little circle in an attempt to keep his balance. "Tell it you straight out. I'll marry your cousin for her money. That will satisfy Sir George. What does he care for anything except that she

214

land a title? And then you and I, my little charmer
. . . we will have an arrangement, just the two of
us. Of course, you must marry, too, to make it all
more convenient. In our circle that sort of thing
is accepted. Or do I mean expected? No matter.
Either way will do."

"Neither way will do, sir!" Kate said in an
outraged voice. "And do not speak to me of 'our
circle.' It is your circle. Your morals. Not mine!"

She thought the force of her declaration would
anger him at the very least, but she was mistaken.
Without warning, Dev caught her in his arms
and kissed her so vigorously that he took her
breath away.

"Release me, sir!" she gasped when her lips
were free. "Release me!" she cried again, when
what she really wanted was to be kept in his
arms forever.

"Release her!" someone shouted, and looking
over Dev's shoulder, Kate saw Fitz approaching
down the gravel path with the speed and grace of
a bolting horse. Before Kate could realize what
was happening, Belinda's suitor was battering
Dev about the head and shoulders. Relinquishing
her at last, the young marquess sank to the
ground, apparently unconscious.

Kate knelt beside him. It was her first impulse
and she followed it. "Oh Fitz!" she cried. "What
have you done?"

"Bravo, young man!" Sir George called from
the upper window. "I would not have thought the
fellow could behave with so much indiscretion.
By gad, there are limits! Marry my daughter for

money, will he? Make my own niece his jade? For shame! Why, I was a scamp when I was young but I took care to protect my honor!"

"We have heard it all, sir!" Lady Prudence exclaimed, coming out of the morning room and bending back her head to address Sir George. "Nanny Benbow is here and has made a mental record of it! If you like, all London will have heard of what took place here by tomorrow evening at the very latest!"

"Papa!" Belinda cried, joining Lady Prudence. "Do you not see how brave Fitz can be? He knows what it is to be a true gentleman! Oh, Papa, please say that he may have a word with you about a most important matter!"

Sir George disappeared inside the room to reappear at the same window, minutes later, with his black horsehair wig set on askew.

"If you insist on it, my dear," he said with a deep sigh, "I see I was wrong about Lord Gilcrest, and no doubt might be be wrong again. I do not have the strength or patience to go through this sort of business another time, damme if I have!"

"Oh, Fitz!" Belinda cried, flying into his outstretched arms. And for the first time in the memory of anyone there, except perhaps his mother, Fitz smiled.

Nineteen

Fitz smiled, but Kate did not. Glad as she was that her uncle had finally capitulated and Belinda would be allowed to marry the man she truly loved, her own sense of loss was so violent as to make her feel weak. For over four years she had lived with a memory and a dream combined. And now the object of those memories, those dreams was lying on the gravel path. Not only had he been too befuddled to defend himself against Fitz's attack, but now he was finding difficulty in raising himself. How she hated to see him like this, overpowered by drink and a gentleman, who in the ordinary way of things would not have been able to touch him, let alone knock him to the ground.

Tears rose to Kate's eyes and she was brushing them away, when Dev, quite without warning, got to his feet and calmly began to brush the gravel from his breeches. And as Kate's eyes moved to his face, she saw that he was smiling. And then, to her utter amazement, he threw back his head and laughed aloud. And he did not laugh alone. Belinda beamed and Fitz grinned, as they stood close together by the white rose-bush. Lady Prudence, still standing just outside the morning room, simpered and made a noise like a rusty gate. Just inside the French windows the old woman cackled cheerfully to her self, and Nell was attacked by a fit of giggles. And from the bedroom, out of the window of which Sir George still leaned, apparently frozen in incredulity, Kate heard Tom raise a great huzza.

"What is this, sir?" Sir George demanded as Fitz and Lord Gilcrest proceeded to shake hands with one another in a companionable fashion. "Will someone tell me what is going on? I have been duped! That much is clear. Everyone one of you stand where you are! No one is to leave this house until I find out who is responsible for this—this outrage."

And with that he withdrew from the window, although he could still be heard cursing Tom, and ordering his man to see to his wig and put him in general order so that he could descend.

"Poor Papa," Belinda said. "What will he do when he discovers we were all in on the plan? All of us except you, Kate. And, as Lord Gilcrest said, it was best to take you by surprise."

"You looked so absolutely outraged, my dear!" Lady Prudence exclaimed. "Why, if it had not been arranged that Fitz would rescue you, I would have done so myself."

"Oh, miss, when you raised your hand to strike his lordship, I was that afraid that you would do so!" Nell declared.

"Well, well," Kate said in a low-pitched voice, her expression thoughtful. "So this was all a ruse?"

She looked at Dev, but he made no answer, although he kept his dark eyes intent on her as though he meant to do nothing now but watch.

"Such clever trickery!" Lady Prudence exclaimed. "I must admit that when you came to see me late last evening, Lord Gilcrest, I was not in a pretty mood. Indeed, it was only the fact that you had a chance to talk to Fitz after taking Belinda and Kate and Sir George home, that gave you the entry to me that was needed. Even when I heard the plan I was not as enthusiastic as Fitz, but he brought me around. And he was right. The old muck-worm was taken in!"

"Have a care, Mama," Fitz said sharply. "You are speaking of the gentleman who is to be my father-in-law, and I will not have any quarreling between you."

"You are not going to become masterful with me, I hope!" Lady Prudence announced, drawing herself up to her full height. "What is it, Nanny? Why are you tugging at my reticule in that peculiar way?"

Nanny Benbow's rosy, wizened face was creased by a toothless smile. "Let the boy be, gel," she said in a creaking voice. "And you, Fitz. Pay your Mama no mind. She always was a bully, even as a gel."

"I hate to interrupt this give and take," Kate said. "But could I ask another question, please?"

"Oh, dear," Belinda cried. "I can tell from your voice that you are angry. When I received that letter about the plan from you this morning, Fitz, I said to Nell: 'Kate may be angry.'"

"La, those were your very words, miss!" Nell exclaimed. "And I said that I thought Miss Kate might flare up at first, but that when she saw all the good . . ."

"I cannot see anything so very *good* about having been publicly made a fool of!" Kate flared. Her brown eyes smoldered like a fire, and every red hair on her head seemed to have a life of its own. "I expect you were all amused to see me taken in by Lord Gilcrest's antics. Pretending to be drunk! Implying that I might be willing to become his mistress! Taking me in his arms and kissing me!"

She paused there, and turned a penetrating stare on Dev who stood, arms akimbo in a defiant fashion, a little to one side.

"Did it amuse you, sir, to play such tricks on a—on a naive, country girl?" she raged.

The others had the good grace to look shamefaced, or at least uncomfortable, but Dev's dark face was expressionless. Still, he started to speak, to answer her. But before he could utter the first word, Sir George burst upon the scene.

"Now I will have my answer!" he announced, coming to rest in the very center of the little garden beside a marble sundial. "Who was responsible for this charade?"

Kate had thought that she could never take her uncle seriously again when she had seen him teaching Belinda how to dance the minuet voluptuously, but he was no longer the unkempt figure who had leaned from the upper window a few minutes ago. Here was a man of substance, a gentleman who should be listened to. Even Lady Prudence made no protest, and Nell, giving a little cry, tried to edge behind a rose-bush.

"The idea was mine, sir," Dev announced in an even voice. "I must apologize for deceiving you, but I will be honest enough to admit that, given the same circumstances, I would do it all again. That is assuming that we can trust you to keep to your word, sir, and allow your daughter to follow her own heart."

"Damme, but you are a pup, sir!" Sir George fumed. "It was a shabby thing to do. Odd rot it, the least I deserve is . . ."

"We are all of us to blame, Papa," Belinda interrupted. "I agreed to bring Kate out here in the garden at a special time, with Nell to help me, if necessary. And Tom was to let Lord Gilcrest in without disturbing you. Lady Prudence was good enough to bring Nanny Benbow with her to act as—witnesses."

"To threaten to make these events public if I should prove recalcitrant, you mean," Sir George retorted. "In case I was not duped sufficently!"

"You will pardon me, sir, if I remind you that if you had not been so difficult to shock as a consequence of your own youthful discretions, it would not have been necessary for me to have gone so far," Lord Gilcrest said. "In a sense it could be said that you are responsible for everything that has happened here this morning, sir, although I for one would not like to make a point of it."

For a moment Kate thought her uncle might be able to fly into a rage and, indeed, she could not have blamed him if he had. For herself, she would have liked to have pounded Dev's chest with both her fists. Were she a man, she would have challenged him. Such easy arrogance was unforgivable.

"Now you *have* done it a bit brown, sir!" Sir George declared and seemed about to throw himself into a rant and rage. But then he took another look at Dev, and began to chuckle. Soon the chuckle turned into a hearty haw-haw and the haw-haw into a roar. Soon he was holding both his sides in an excess of hilarity.

"Well, well," he sputtered finally. "All's fair in love and war, they say, and no harm's done. What a scoundrel you are, Dev! I might as well take off my hat to you, and would do it here and now if I were wearing one."

"Oh, you are as bad as he is!" Kate told her uncle impatiently. "No harm done! And your own niece treated like a jade. Well, I will have no more of it! Nell will help me pack my bags and I can be in the country by five if there is still time for me to take the post chaise."

"You will arrive home all the quicker, Miss Harrison, if you will travel down to Kent with me in my phaeton," Lord Gilcrest said before anyone else could speak. "In order to be completely proper, Miss Robinson might accompany you."

"La, he is such a gentleman, that one!" Nell could be heard exclaiming.

"But Kate, I cannot let you go!" Belinda cried, running to embrace her friend, while Fitz, whose hand she continued to hold, observed that it would be a pity to leave just now with a wedding coming up, and Nanny Benbow cupped one lace-mittened hand to her ear in order not to miss a word.

"You have a singular sense of humor, sir," Kate replied. "Still, if it amuses you to harrass me, I suppose I must endure it."

Throwing back her head distainfully and scooping up her skirts, she removed herself from her cousin's embrace and started up the walk, hoping that she had had the satisfaction of the last word at least. But when she reached the windows which let into the morning room, she found Dev beside her.

"I am making no joke of it, Miss Harrison," he said quietly. "I mean to go to the country to have a word with your father, although I would like your permission first."

"My father!" Kate exclaimed. "What business have you with him, sir?"

"If you would think a bit, you might guess," Dev said in such a low voice that Nanny Benbow was in a perfect agony trying to hear him. "I mean to ask for his consent to try to win you."

Kate stared at him incredulously.

"And I mean to be quite honest," Dev went on. "If fair means do not succeed; then I will turn to foul. For I intend to be quite unscrupulous, and it is only right that you be warned as well."

His eyes were so intense that Kate could not look away. She wanted to be outraged but her anger seemed to have fled somewhere. And, when Dev's mouth curled in a slow smile, she felt all her defenses crumble. Vaguely, she was aware that the others had withdrawn into the house. Indeed, she saw her uncle place one finger to his lips as he ushered Lady Prudence through the morning room and out into the hall.

"I can make all sorts of promises," Dev murmured against her cheeks, for somehow, without her knowing how, they had moved very close to one another.

"For example?" Kate whispered.

"I will never ask you to remove my boots," he told her fondly. "And if, through any set of circumstances, you were to find your face quite covered with mud, I promise not to laugh."

With a contented smile, Kate let herself be drawn into a long embrace. Later there would be time to hedge a bit, to make him fret and worry, for she was determined that things must not come to him too easily. And later they could discuss his friends and the quite scandalous way he had foxed Sir George . . . And then his lips touched hers, and for the time at least, all Kate's good intentions were forgotten.